0586783

THE SPECTER

(WAXWOOD SERIES: BOOK 1)

TAM MAY

THE SPECTER

WAXWOOD SERIES: BOOK 1

Tam May

The Specter
Waxwood Series: Book 1
Tam May

Published by Dreambook Press.

Click or visit:
https://www.tammayauthor.com

Cover Design © 2021 by Essi/100 Covers

ISBN: 978-09981979-4-4 (Print)
ISBN: 978-09981979-5-1 (ebook)

Quotes in the text are as follows:

Chapter 1, Chapter 4, and Chapter 7

Patmore Coventry, *The Angel in the House*, Canto IV, The Morning Call, Preludes, I. The Rose of the World

Chapter 30

Lord Byron, "She Walks In Beauty"

Chapter 38

King James Version of the Bible, Matthew 7:15

Chapter 43

Robert Browning, "Life in a Love"

DEDICATION

To Aila and Becky for their encouragement and support of my work.

TABLE OF CONTENTS

PROLOGUE

 ant more feisty Gilded Age heroines who go against conventions? Love intricate mysteries with humor and a fun cast of characters? Then you'll love my free offer at the end of this book! So don't forget to check that out when you get to the end. Happy reading!

THE FIRST TIME Vivian walked into the House of Colston, she was intimidated by the scent of roses. Vases of tea roses in mauve, red, and white sat on small tables neatly laid out with women's accessories. Their sweet scent filled the velvet room with its tall, frosted windows with an impenetrable mist. She pressed her hands to her forehead.

Her grandmother put her arm around her shoulders. "Come, darling." She said in a commanding tone, "Who is the proprietor of this establishment?"

A woman stepped forward. "I am, madame."

"May we open a window, please?"

Vivian felt her intimidation worsen as she looked at the lady whose countenance was as haughty as her mother's.

"Madame, that isn't possible. The dust —"

"My granddaughter is about to be one of your best clients." Grandmother spoke with even more dignity. "I suppose you can open one window for her."

"Yes, madame." The woman obliged by sliding open a sliver the window furthest from the street.

"Oh, surely, you can do better than that."

Vivian could almost sense Grandmother's satisfaction as the woman opened the window further, frowning all the while.

"Market Street isn't very busy just now," Vivian chimed in. "I suppose the horses won't kick up too much mud on your lovely curtains."

"You are right, mademoiselle." She bowed. "Shall I bring you a glass of water?" She sounded less haughty.

"If I could only sit down —" Vivian dropped into one of the stuffed chairs.

"Certainly, mademoiselle," said Mrs. Colston. "I would be more than happy to help you when you've recovered."

"We're waiting for someone," said Grandmother. Although she wasn't very tall, she stood with the dignity inbred in her since her own debutante days.

"Certainly, madame." The woman bowed.

"In the meantime, we'll take a look at that rack," Grandmother pointed to the corner with her parasol.

"But madame!" The woman looked slightly horrified. "Those are last year's models. I keep them as samples only."

"Then we shall see your samples." Grandmother waved her off with an elegant flap of her gloved hand.

"Yes, madame." The woman withdrew behind an embossed door, again with the deep frown.

Vivian, now feeling more herself, joined her grandmother at the wooden rack heavily weighed down by bejeweled and embossed gowns. She idly flipped through muted purple and orange, blue and yellow, and gold and cream. She could envision herself standing at the doorway of the Alderdice Hall ballroom receiving guests for her coming out ball, her shoulders and waist weighed down by such a dazzling gown, looking more triumphant than happy.

"I suppose I'll need to make a show of myself," she mumbled.

"What, darling?" Grandmother glanced at her.

"I was thinking of the ball," she said. "Must I make a show of myself?"

Her grandmother looked amused. "A debutante usually does at her own coming out."

"But everyone there knows me," she protested. "They've known me since I was a child."

"Exactly," Grandmother said. "When you were a child. You're almost a lady now, Vivian. And being a lady changes one." There was a wistful look in her usually sparkling eyes.

"I don't think it will change me," Vivian said.

Her grandmother looked grave "It will, darling. It always does"

"Why?" Vivian asked.

"A lady has expectations," she said.

Vivian looked away. "I'm not afraid of that. Mother's made my expectations clear since the day I was born!"

"Yes, I suppose she has," said her grandmother. She was holding up a dress of brilliant green silk with delicate lace inlay.

Mrs. Colston, who had been lingering nearby with her hands behind her back, said, "That's the emerald dress, madame. Jewel shades are still the rage." She sounded hopeful.

"I've always loved this shade of green," said Grandmother.

Vivian stared at her. "You never wear it."

Her grandmother smiled ruefully and let the dress fall from her hands, swinging on the hanger. "No, perhaps I don't."

"You should, Grandmother." Vivian took her arm. "It would make you look divine. But you always do. Never a hair out of place."

"Never a hair out of place," Grandmother murmured. Then, in a distressed tone, she added, "But it wasn't always like that! It wasn't always like that!"

Vivian felt the alarm ringing in her bones. Lately it seemed Grandmother had shifts from the calm and collected person she knew to a bird flapping around in a cage, trying to get out.

"We have silk emerald this year," Mrs. Colston prompted.

"Green is the color of the forest. It's wild, free, and always growing." Grandmother's eyes were misty. "A young man said that to me once."

"If madame would like to make an appointment for the young lady's fitting —"

Just then, the door slid open and Larissa walked in. Vivian observed her mother's swan-like grace as if she had been taught to cultivate decorum over kindness. And, indeed, Larissa could be stern and even cruel at times.

But it was clear Mrs. Colston was impressed by her regal appearance, as she glanced behind her at the two assistants lingering near the mirrors as if warning them to be on their best behavior.

Larissa peeled off her gloves and placed her parasol carefully on the stand. "I'm sorry I'm late, Mother," she said to Grandmother. "Father had some errands for me to do."

"And his errands always come first," Vivian mumbled, "even before his own granddaughter's debutante ball gown."

"You've become altogether too impertinent lately, Vivian," Larissa snapped, settling on a couch.

"When one is a lady, Mother, one may say what she likes." Vivian sniffed.

"Only if she can get away with it, darling," Grandmother murmured, and they both laughed.

But Larissa found it less than amusing. "This is serious, Vivian. I expect you to help me instruct her, Mother." She gave her mother a wary look.

This seemed to return Grandmother to her less vivid self, and she slowly lowered herself in a chair.

Larissa looked at Mrs. Colston. "I made an appointment for a fitting for my daughter, Vivian. I'm Larissa Alderdice."

"But of course, madame!" The woman looked pleased. "We are honored by your patronage. I have the models all ready."

Vivian glanced at the wooden rack with the emerald dress still swinging on the hanger.

"That won't be necessary," Larissa said. The two shop assistants, who had come forward at their employer's summons, back away. "We only want to see a pink dress. Rose-colored, to be more exact."

"Mother, you can be serious!" Vivian stared at her.

"It will wash her out, Larissa," Grandmother said softly. "Pink on a strawberry blond."

"Rose-colored," Larissa repeated, her voice certain.

Vivian's stomach grew tight. "I don't want to make a show of myself, but I don't want to be invisible either."

"Remember what I told you last week, dear," said her mother. "Alderdice women always wear rose at their coming out."

"I think she ought to be able to chose the color, Larissa," Grandmother's voice rose. "It is her dress, after all."

"It's the family tradition, Mother." Larissa eyed Vivian. "You've seen that portrait of your grandmother, haven't you?"

Vivian thought of the picture hanging in the upstairs parlor of Alderdice Hall.

"Oh, but that was a different time," Grandmother's voice fluttered. "Girls were expected — well, we didn't argue over such things."

"And neither will Vivian," said Larissa. "She will do as she's told."

Vivian felt ill. "I think the green would suit me better."

"Green would look vulgar," Larissa snapped. "I can't imagine what gave you such an idea. Or whom."

Her eyes slid in the general direction of where Grandmother stood. Vivian watched as Grandmother placed a pince-nez to her eyes and pretended to examine a pair of gloves on the table next to her. But she could see tears gathering in the corners of the older woman's now dulled eyes.

"Am I'm to disappear into the bright lights and white marble on the most important day of my life?" Vivian tried to steady her voice. Larissa put her hand on her shoulder. "You'll get plenty of attention after the ball, dear, believe me. Come now." She smiled. "Your grandmother wore rose and so did I. Your grandfather will expect it."

"Yes." Grandmother's voice was barely audible. "He'll expect it. He likes ladies in pink."

It was as if she were a gas lamp that had been burning its crystal light for years but was now nothing but a milky shadow. Remembering the vibrance of the woman in the portrait that was Penelope Alderdice, the tears came to Vivian's eyes.

CHAPTER 1

*H*er mother was right. Attention turned on Vivian after her debutant ball, more than she could stand. The parties, picnics, boating excursions, and theater openings molded together like clay into one shapeless form of faces she couldn't remember and conversations that meant nothing. That first year, she fell into bed every night, or sometimes in the early morning, longing for the quiet life she had had of books, walks, and meaningful chats with her grandmother before she had put on that awful rose-colored ball gown.

Although Grandmother remained a shadowy figure throughout while Larissa and Grandfather took over, it was her grandmother who saved her from the whirlwind of forgotten faces and empty conversations when she died in the summer of 1892.

Vivian read her obituary in the paper at breakfast:

Penelope Alderdice (*ne* Carlyle).

-On the 17th of October 1892, **Penelope**, wife of shipping magnate **Malcolm Alderdice**, died peacefully at the age of 59 in her home on Nob Hill. Mrs. Alderdice was a celebrated socialite and benevolent lady and will be greatly missed in this city. She will be buried on the 19th at Mountain View Cemetery in Oakland. Services will be conducted by Reverend Robert Norris and take place at the Alderdice Hall chapel. Attendance is invitation only. Mrs. Alderdice is survived by her husband, daughter, and two grandchildren.

"Pure dignity, composure, ease,
Declare affections nobly fix'd,
And impulse sprung from due degrees
Of sense and spirit sweetly mix'd;"

Jake's face went limp as he laid down the paper and stared down at his lap in silence. Vivian knew he was trying to fight back tears. His youth and his devotion to their grandmother made him vulnerable to the grief their mother and grandfather successfully suppressed under the heavy layer of Alderdice dignity and pride.

"I wish you hadn't, Mother," she said softly.

Larissa looked up from the letter in her hand. "Hadn't what?"

"Given the papers that quote." She pushed back the warm plate of eggs. "It sounds so disingenuous."

Her mother looked alarmed. "It was your grandmother's favorite poem."

"It's Grandfather's favorite poem," Jake said quietly.

Grandfather's head shot up. "Angel, my angel, angel in the house!"

"Yes, Father, she was an angel," said Larissa. "I see Doreen burned the toast again this morning." She pulled the bell cord.

"Why must the service take place in the chapel?"

"Your grandmother would have wished it," said Larissa.

Her brother gave her a sly look. "No, she wouldn't."

"That's enough, Jacob!"

"Grandmother believed it was haunted,"

"Don't be ridiculous." Larissa snapped "There are no ghosts in this house."

"I didn't say it was haunted with ghosts, Mother," he said. "It was built on sacrilegious ground."

Vivian stared at him. "How do you know?"

"He's only trying to frighten us," her mother assured.

Ignoring her, Vivian asked, "Who told you about the chapel, Jake?"

"Grandmother. Before she died."

Larissa sighed. "Your grandmother said things toward the end. That's why I couldn't let you see her often. She was — well, not exactly in her right mind."

"She was always in her right mind!" Jake snarled.

Her mother picked up the letter opener without answering.

"What do you mean, it was built on sacrilegious ground?" Vivian asked.

"The architect went outside for a smoke one night, and the face of a vixen appeared on the ground as he was lighting his cigar."

"Nonsense," said Larissa. "Children were playing nearby and drew pictures in the dirt. Isn't that so, Father?"

"Pests, all of them, run, run, run!" Grandfather growled.

"I don't think he knows what we're talking about," Vivian said.

"The picture wasn't there when he went out, Mother," Jake ventured. "It appeared with the light of his match."

"Finish your breakfast, Jacob. And stop telling wicked tales."

This seething command prompted him to pick up the fork, but he he put it down again after a few bites.

Grandfather's daze disappeared just as quickly as it had come, and Vivian heard him take a deep breath, a sign he was about to make a speech. "Damned superstitious, that man, but your grand-mother believed him. She thought the chapel would take care of the bad omen. What nonsense! Did it for her, though. That dome and those windows cost a fortune, but, by God, she wanted it and she got it!" His chest heaved out. "I always gave her everything she wanted."

"Of course you did," Larissa said with a soft smile.

The affirmation snatched away his moment of clarity, and his face was once more a mask of confusion. There was no more conversation during the rest of the meal.

~~~~~

Later that day, after her mother returned from the undertakers, she and Vivian retreated to the study to answer more condolences. The weight of melancholy returned as Vivian sat on the couch with telegrams and notes spread around her. Grandfather wandered in and, although Larissa spoke to him, he seemed not to hear her. He stared at the drawn curtains shadowing the pleasant peach and white hues.

She and her mother went on with their work with only the scraping of unfolding paper and the scrape of the fountain pen echoing in the quiet room with an occasional cough from Grandfather.

"The Taylors wrote us a very nice note, Father." Larissa held up a card.

"Yes, what?" He gaped at her.

"The Taylors, darling." Her mother's voice rose a few notches. "We were just talking about them last night. Do you want me to order you some coffee?"

His fingers gathered as if he were holding a cup and saucer in his hands, his eyes narrowing. Larissa reached for the bell cord.

"I don't think we should tell people the chapel is haunted," Vivian remarked as she tore open another envelope. "The Washington blue bloods are as superstitious as anybody."

"There is nothing to tell because it's not haunted," her mother insisted.

"Vixen in the dust, vixen in the dust," Grandfather threw his head back as if he were going to laugh. But no sound came out.

"Perhaps Grandmother had the chapel built to protect us from bad omens," Vivian said.

Her mother was no longer listening. She was reading a note,

and her face, previously impassive with the business of corre-spondence, grew pallid.

"What is it?" Vivian peered at her.

She threw the note on the table. "What impertinence! What gall!"

The paper was as rough and plain as the envelope. There was no family emblem and no heading. The writing was neither light-handed nor curvy like other condolences Vivian had been read-ing. "It isn't from one of our friends, is it?"

"Certainly not!"

"Who is it from, then?"

"See for yourself." Larissa reached for the coffee pot Basset had brought in.

Vivian read:

Dear Mrs. Alderdice,

You don't know me though I feel as if you ought to. I was your mother's friend here in Waxwood. Indeed, oh, indeed, our fathers grew up together. Your mother and I were debutantes together, and Grace even gave me a picture for my 20th birthday, oh, it was very sweet and a little forlorn — but no matter.

I cannot express how heartbroken I was when I heard she was dead. Oh, how one forgets the years of one's youth, yes, one forgets. Or one puts them away like locks of hair from a beloved one knows will never return.

What must you think of me! I go off here and there now that I am old. My daughter Ruthie, she has such patience with me. Waxwood is the sort of place where one may lose one's measure. One may even lose oneself in an adventure! Grace certainly did. But she was never really lost, was she, for she had me and Mama and Papa and Loretta and oh, so many of us who loved her. No, indeed, she was not lost. She was only misplaced. Or is that losing oneself as well? Well, no matter.

I read the funeral is invitation only, but you will allow us to come to the funeral, I'm sure. Grace and I were such good friends. Surely, a fine lady such as yourself would not deny an old woman who goes off now and then that last sanction.

Remind me to your father.

Bertha Ross

"An odd letter," Vivian murmured.

"Odd is putting it mildly, dear. It's a crank, a hoax of some sort." Larissa slid the sugar bowl back on the tray. "One is apt to encounter such people when there is a death in the family."

"You don't know who she is, then?"

Her mother leaned sideways a little so her ankles peered out from under the skirt of her dress. They were well covered, but their angularity strained the leather casing of the shoes she wore. Vivian recognized the sign. Her mother was trying to reestablish her equilibrium. "I've never heard the name before."

"Grandfather?" Vivian peered at him.

"Leave him alone!" The order cut into the darkened room.

"Why does she call Grandmother 'Grace'?" she asked.

"Because she's mad," her mother insisted.

"No," Vivian said. "No, I believe she's sincere." She placed the note on the table.

Larissa grimaced. "Fools are always sincere."

"Where is Waxwood?"

"Stop asking so many questions, Vivian." Her mother reached for her fountain pen. "We can't have her coming to the funeral."

"Bad luck, bad luck," Grandfather murmured.

"It certainly is, Father," Larissa said. "Bad luck to have a madwoman at a funeral."

Vivian eyed her. "Superstition can't touch the Alderdices, remember?"

"Please, dear." Larissa's steady tone held a cutting edge.

Vivian watched as her mother leaned forward and scribbled a brief note. She pulled the bell cord. When Basset appeared, she thrust it at him. "Please send someone to deliver this as soon as possible."

"No reply, ma'am?"

"No reply."

When he was gone, Vivian said, "You're in rather a hurry to answer her, aren't you, Mother?"

"The funeral *is* tomorrow." Larissa gathered the rest of the envelopes. "She must not come."

Vivian felt her pulse rise. "It's rather cruel of you to refuse this poor woman the right to pay her last respects."

"I told you, dear, it's all a hoax. A terrible hoax!"

Vivian had never seen her mother so nervous. Her forehead was damp, and her shoulders looked as if they had frozen into a shrug. "What harm could there be in her coming?" she asked.

"Bad luck, bad luck!" Grandfather was off again, his hand in sword position.

"Don't upset yourself, Father," said Larissa.

"Perhaps it would be bad luck," Vivian said. "But not because she's a madwoman or a fool."

Her mother rose. "See that you finish your duties, Vivian." She placed the rest of the unopened envelopes on the couch. "And send for Basset to see to your grandfather, will you, dear? I believe he's quite tired."

When Larissa had left the room, Vivian looked at him. "Do you know who Bertha Ross is, Grandfather?"

He had gone bewildered again, but Vivian saw his eyes were alert.

Her mother had left Bertha Ross' note lying on the table. Vivian placed it back in its envelope, folded it, and slipped it up her sleeve.

CHAPTER 2

*V*ivian sat at the end of the family pew. Her skin crawled underneath the heavy taffeta as Washington Street's blue bloods filed in, their eyes falling on the family with a mixture of curiosity and regret. The chapel was immaculate, and the stained glass windows so polished one would have thought they held services there every Sunday. She avoided looking at the casket with its embellished lid, grateful her mother had not insisted it be open during the service.

Larissa sat beside her completely wrapped in black silk crepe, every recognizable feature of her face and figure carefully concealed. The grenadine veil her mother had chosen draped over her head down to her breast so nothing was visible to anyone standing even a little distance away from her. Vivian knew the veil did not conceal melancholy or emotional overwhelm, but a determined hardness. Each angular feature was molded and impassive so as to resemble a black phantom.

Next to her mother sat Jake and then Grandfather. Though he had no veil to hide behind, every part of her grandfather solidified and guarded him from judgment. Vivian wondered of whose judgment he was most afraid — God's or the Washington Street blue bloods.

A whispering rain rolled steadily down the windows. Vivian glanced out, watching droplets pool into the etchings of angels and birds, making them look as if they were weeping. Grandmother had always loved the way the angels merged into the birds and the birds embraced the angels. "Heaven must be a contented place if angels and birds may entwine," she had said. The sight of them touched Vivian so deeply she had to bite her lip to keep tears from washing over her face.

Her mother leaned over and said in a low voice, "Control yourself, dear."

Vivian choked out, "The entire neighborhood is here but no one is weeping."

"One needn't shed tears to feel remorse or even sadness," Larissa pointed out.

"It's all so refined, isn't it?" Vivian let out a gasp. "Behold the pillars of Far Western society. I read that in the *Chronicle* once,"

"So we are, dear, so we are." Her mother pulled her veil closer to her face.

"They aren't here to mourn." Vivian's voice shook. "They came to see and be seen."

"Don't be rude, Vivian."

"Remember when Mr. Harvey's mother died?" Vivian asked. "The Harveys invited the *Sun* and the *Chronicle* to the cemetery!"

"We are not the Harveys." Larissa's voice cut like a razor blade.

"Oh, heavens, no. We're much more dignified," Vivian sniffed. "We're practically royalty."

Several ladies from the Washington Street Benevolent Society made their way down the aisle, nodding at Larissa in a pensive way. They were all decked out in the season's best fashion, though the dark colors befitted the occasion.

"They might just as well be attending a garden party," Vivian muttered.

"Remember," her mother whispered, "they're our friends."

Vivian stared at the veiled head. "I almost believe you approve."

Larissa took her hand and pressed it hard. "They're here and that's what's important." Vivian could almost feel the smirk behind the black grenadine.

"I see," she said slowly. "Fashionable mourning is better than no mourning, is that it?"

Her mother silenced her as Reverend Norris approached the pulpit. Just as the general shuffling died down, the chapel doors opened and a stout woman appeared crowned in sunlight. Heads turned and pews creaked as people craned their necks to see who dared arrive late. As the woman moved out of the glare, Vivian saw she was not stout but looked it only because she sat in a wheelchair. A tall, slim woman about Larissa's age stood behind her.

"Who on earth is that?" Vivian looked at her mother.

Larissa did not answer, peeing through the veil and narrowing her eyes to get a better look.

The reverend ceased leafing through his Bible and looked at her mother. All heads were turned to the front of the chapel now.

Larissa rose and went down the side aisle with Vivian at her heels.

"The daughter!" the woman exclaimed. "Oh, you don't look like your mother at all."

Larissa stepped toward the open doors. "I'm sorry, but this is a private service."

The younger woman regarded her with a severe look. "Your mother was Penelope Alderdice, wasn't she?"

"Yes."

"We came to mourn," she said. "If you'll kindly show us where we may take our places —"

"This is a private service," Larissa repeated.

The elderly woman chirped, "We've come all the way from Waxwood."

Vivian's heart raced as she thought of the desk drawer where she had hidden the letter from the day before. "Mother," she whispered, "I believe this is Bertha Ross."

Her mother stiffened, but her tone was calm. "I made myself clear when I answered your note yesterday, Mrs. Ross."

"Oh, but you didn't mean it, you couldn't have meant it, no, indeed!"

Larissa's voice dropped. "I would be most obliged if you would leave."

Vivian grabbed her arm. "Mother, it's a sin to turn mourners away!"

She had spoken too loudly. More heads turned, and low murmurings rang through the chapel. A voice in the back exclaimed, "I don't care who they are! Larissa oughtn't to turn them away if they came to pay their respects." Others hissed in agreement.

He mother stepped forward, her skirt swinging wide to reveal the ankle. "Come this way." She led them to an empty pew in the last row. The younger woman wheeled her mother into the aisle and sat down, her hands folded in her lap.

Vivian could not see her mother's face hidden in the heavy veil, but she could feel rage vibrating from her as she walked like a soldier. Grandfather stared, his forehead peaked with annoyance. Jake's eyes, widened like a wondering child as he leaned back to catch a glimpse of the two newcomers. Grandfather clamped his hand on his shoulder, and his attention returned to the pulpit.

"Intruders!" Grandfather hissed as she and her mother sat down.

"Don't upset yourself, Father." Larissa picked up her Bible.

Vivian glanced at the corner of the chapel, thinking Bertha

Ross and her daughter had more right to be there than the Nob Hill aristocrats who filled the pews more with their curiosity than their grief.

There was a brief silence as the reverend cleared his throat. Vivian's eyes stung with tears, and she slipped her hand under her own veil to wipe them away. Her gaze went to Bertha Ross. She noticed the woman's dark blue muslin and the dainty lace collar lopsided around her neck, as if she had sewn it on herself. Mrs. Ross did not wear a veil, so her face looked bald with anguish. If Jake were to make a drawing of the woman now, he would title it "Woman in Proper Mourning." The vacant stare and sagging figure belonged to one remembering an old friend. Despite what Larissa said the day before, Vivian felt sure Mrs. Ross had known her grandmother, perhaps known her well.

Her eyes fell on the younger woman, no doubt the "Ruthie" of the letter. She sat upright, frozen with purpose in the same simple dress as her mother. It was clear she did not want to be there but had come out of duty or promise. And yet, her grave countenance embraced the occasion as if she had known Penelope Alderdice as intimately as her mother.

The organ began a hymn and a cough escaped from the front pew. Grandfather always coughed to hide an unbridled moment of sorrow or pain escaping his towering figure. Mrs. Ross' head snap, her gaze alert. The elderly woman's startled eyes grew dim and narrow.

Miss Ross was looking anxiously at her mother, and her hand reached out to the shawl draped over her shoulders as if to adjust it. But then they went back into her lap without having touched the coarse fabric.

Vivian leaned forward with a mad urge to approach the Rosses. She felt a pinch on her arm, the smarting touch of her mother's admonition. Vivian relaxed and began counting fingers. It was a habit she had come by as a child, counting the fingers of one hand up and down and then the other. Thumb one, two, three on down, then back up again like a pianist practicing scales.

Reverend Norris had reached one of his screeching peaks. "Penelope Alderdice had great tolerance and angelic patience. God saw fit to make her the silent and graceful partner of one of our city's great industrialists."

Every gaze fell upon her grandfather. His lips curved with a satisfied smile. His arms tensed, and Vivian thought for a horrifying moment he was going to rise and take a bow.

"In the words of Mr. Patmore, 'Her disposition is devout/Her countenance angelic'—"

A small cry came from the back of the chapel. Vivian's hands dug into the wooden pew. Heads turned and the hollow silence filled with sniffing and murmur.

"Why, she's sobbing! Sobbing as if her heart were broken!"

"Well, really, no self-control!"

"Not from here, not one of us."

Mrs. Ross' face was damp with tears and her figure shook with loud sobs. Vivian rose, gathering her skirt about her.

"What are you doing?" her mother hissed.

"I mean to help her." Vivian took a step into the aisle, but Larissa grabbed her arm.

"Don't be a fool! We're in the middle of service."

Jake placed his hand on top of his mother's. "Mother, let her go."

"Keep silent!"

He sank into his seat.

"She's the only one who really cares, Mother." Vivian's voice broke.

"Please, dear, you're making a scene." Larissa's eyes darted.

"I don't care!" Vivian's voice rang through the chapel.

A few ladies in the front row gasped. Her mother put her arms around her. "Your compassion is touching, dear. Her daughter is taking care of her. You see?"

Miss Ross was speaking to her mother in a low voice. Mrs. Ross seemed calmer, but gloom and despair showed on her face.

The reverend continued, and Vivian heard Larissa murmur, "I hope that woman hasn't unnerved Father."

Grandfather's slanted blue eyes were vague and wide, looking at Reverend Norris as he expounded on Penelope Alderdice's saintly qualities. Vivian thought he almost looked confused as to whom the reverend was referring. What a different man he was from the man he had been only a few weeks before!

The service ended, and the general shuffle began. Vivian watched as people shook hands with their friends just as they did after every church service on Sundays. Her eyes tilted to the corner of the chapel. Mrs. Ross sat with her head buried in her hands.

~~~~~

They returned from the cemetery subdued, but when they entered the doors of Alderdice Hall, Larissa immediately went to work with the servants to arrange the upstairs parlor to receive mourners.

The room was filled with mirrors, now all covered to prevent the reflection of the dead. Swathed on all sides by velvet and crepe, she feared she would disappear inside the folds. "Mother, it feels like a crypt in here." She shivered.

Larissa lifted her veil over her head. "Stop being so morbid, Vivian."

"That's rather ironic, isn't it?" Vivian's tone was wary. "Since it's a morbid occasion."

Larissa did not answer, but turned to Basset and the footmen to disburse instructions.

Vivian fanned herself as discreetly as she could, trying to breath in the stifling room . She wondered whether her mother was afraid Grandmother's soul would walk into a mirror and remain there, or her spirit would appear at a window, pointing a finger at her daughter, accusing her of—what? Grandmother had taken care to be pleasantly silent during her life. She would hardly hurl accusations in death. And yet, Larissa seemed afraid that this is exactly what she would do. But what accusations could Grandmother have against them now?

The footmen dispatched to light the gaslights, candles, and candelabras, and as the room begin to absorb the light, Vivian noticed one picture had not been turned to the wall. The portrait of her grandmother painted soon after her coming out gazed down at her. Vivian had always loved it because the pale pink shades of her taffeta ball gown and pearls suited her so well. Her mother kept the portrait well-preserved, but in the milky light of the room, her grandmother's face looked worn and dusty, the flushed cheeks and lips faded.

Vivian wandered over to the painting and read the gold plaque on the frame: *In mind and manners how discreet!/How artless in her very art.* She recognized the same epitaph was on Grandmother's gravestone. The woman in the picture languishing on the *tête-à-tête* which now stood in the corner of this very room in her rose-colored dress did indeed look like the epitome of discretion and artlessness.

Grandfather sidled up beside her. For a moment, his dazed expression gave way to the crusty, stoic face she had known in childhood. His eyes fell upon her and the same bewilderment she had seen too often since her grandmother's death returned. "Patmore is the maker of veritable angels." He pointed at the plaque.

Her mother took Grandfather's arm. "Come, Father. Vivian, remember your duty to *all*, not a select few."

Vivian, feeling the dig for her earlier solicitation of the Rosses, saluted. "I shall do my duty as our docile clanswomen before me."

"Don't be flippant," her mother snapped just as a rustle of skirts sounded from the doorway hailed the Millers

"Oh, it's *so* unfortunate!" As if on cue, Beatrice and Emma produced black handkerchiefs in their clutched hands.

"The cycle of life, they say," Beatrice continued amidst a discomforting silence.

"Penelope was always — always—" Emma heaved a sob.

"—a kind and generous woman," her mother finished.

"I was going to say *loyal* and dependable," Her daughter breathed. "Even with those most trying to her patience." Her eyes slid at Grandfather.

"Yes, yes," Larissa murmured.

"A kind soul," Beatrice glanced at Vivian as if looking for affirmation.

"A kind soul," Vivian mumbled.

"We were all *so* grateful she came back," Beatrice said with a sigh. "We weren't sure she would, you know."

"Came back?" Vivian echoed.

"We've brought out the Whistler sherry, dear." Larissa placed her hand on Beatrice's arm and guided her toward the waiting tray. "I know how much you adore it."

Grandfather's eyes glazed glazed over, and his stick thrust out at them as they passed, more protective than threatening. Vivian's eyes followed his to the two women helping themselves to sherry glasses. Beatrice's words echoed through the stifling room: *We were so grateful she came back.* "I thought Grandmother disliked travel," Vivian whispered.

Larissa took her hand and pressed it hard. "People say the oddest things at funerals. Take no notice, dear."

She had no time to ask any more questions, as the mourners began to arrive. People took her hand, murmuring empty words of sorrow and regret. Vivian nodded and mumbled her thanks at their condolences for the angel in the house they had known. Not one of them had really known Grandmother behind the mask of social grace and propriety. They had no idea Grandmother had loathed traveling. Neither were they aware she had loved wild poppies, redwoods, and, for some inexplicable reason, fish.

As the line dwindled, Bertha Ross and her daughter appeared. Up close, Vivian could see the woman's face sagged with tears as she stared openly at Vivian, taking her hand. The leathery skin warmed Vivian's. "I knew your grandmother, yes, I knew her."

Larissa put her hand on Mrs. Ross' shoulder. "I realize you came here in good faith, and I shall not object —"

"Not in front of your friends, you mean," Miss Ross mumbled.

Larissa ignored this. "We have a very good sherry over there." She nodded toward one of the tables.

Vivian grasped the woman's hand steadily in hers. "May I bring you a glass, Mrs. Ross?"

"Oh, heavens, call me Bertha!" A small peal of laughter escaped the wide lips. "Grace always thought Bertha too old-fashioned. I suppose it is."

"Why do you call my grandmother 'Grace'?"

The woman blinked. "Why, she preferred it."

Larissa's sharp eyes pointed like arrows. "My mother's name is Penelope."

"Oh, but she changed it in Waxwood," Bertha's eyes grew damp. "We never knew why. I'd like to know why, yes, indeed, I'd like to know even now." She gave Larissa the same open stare she had given Vivian. "Do *you* know why?"

Vivian had never seen her mother's so clammy and devout of its angular features. Larissa murmured, "Why did she have to come? I *told* her not to come."

Vivian grabbed the small, wrinkled claw. "Come, Bertha, I'll get you a glass of sherry and you can tell me all about Grace."

"Vivian!"

"Yes, yes, call me Bertha," the woman lamented. "And my daughter is Ruth."

"You call me Vivian, won't you?" She smiled at them both. "And my brother is Jake."

"Vivian." Her mother's threatening tone made her stomach turn.

"Why, Mother," she said. "You told me to do my duty. Jake and I will both do our duty, won't we?" She looked at her brother, who had appeared net to her. Jake drew back from the elderly woman, his eyes intent on their mother.

Larissa cleared her throat. "Jacob, I think your grandfather needs you."

He wavered for a moment. Without looking at Vivian, he went back to the room where Grandfather was standing near a crowd of people.

A woman whom Vivian recognized as Mrs. Bilton, the leader of the Ladies Auxiliary, came forward. "Anything wrong, dear?" She peered at Larissa.

"No, of course not." Larissa tried to smile. "Vivian is so anxious to making everyone feel comfortable, she sometimes forgets herself."

"You're such a kind-hearted creature, Vivian, just like your grandmother." Mrs. Bilton nodded. "In times like these, we all need kindness."

The approval in the woman's eyes was so bald, Vivian knew her mother would no longer protest, so she took firm hold of Bertha's arm as Ruth wheeled her around.

CHAPTER 3

*V*ivian led the Rosses to the *tête-à-tête* Grandmother had insisted they keep in the parlor more out of amusement than sentiment. She once told Vivian how she had sat on the *tête-à-tête* in her coming out days when young men came calling while Great-Grandmother stationed herself in a discreet but visible corner listening to her engaged in innocuous conversation with the gentleman. When Vivian asked if Grandfather was one of those young men, Grandmother murmured, "He had more daring ways."

"I haven't had sherry in, oh, I don't know how long!" Bertha said.

Vivian handed both women a tiny glass and settled on the rug in front of Bertha. "I don't think I ever heard Grandmother mention Waxwood when she spoke of her travels as a young woman."

"The little town by the little bay." Bertha giggled. "Why, the trees aren't even in the town!"

"Trees?"

"The wax wood trees! Mercy, child, it was so long ago." The woman sighed. "Most of our fathers were fishermen at one time or another. I suppose Grace's was too, though he left when he was a young man."

"When you say 'our,' who do you mean?"

Jake suddenly appeared, his hands still woven behind his back. He glanced about with a nervous eye, and Vivian imagined he had barely escaped their grandfather's stern watch.

The woman gazed up at him with a smile. "What a lovely boy. You were Grace's favorite, weren't you?"

"Please forgive Mama," Ruth intervened. "She can be far too blunt at times."

"As a matter of fact, he was Grandmother's favorite," Vivian said. "How did you know?"

"Oh, he reminded me of, well—" Her hands grasped the sherry, though she did not drink it. "You asked me something before. I've forgotten."

"Vivian asked who were the fishermen's daughters, Mama," her daughter prompted.

"Why, yes. Grace, Laura, Mary, Patricia, Selma, and myself, of course. The Waxwood Belles." She chuckled. "We may not have had big city fineries, but we never smelled of fish, no, never!"

Vivian bit her lip to keep from smiling from showing to mourners gathered near them. Jake covered his mouth as if to cough, but she imagined he was hiding a smile too.

Bertha did not miss this and burst out into pealing laughter. A small hush fell over the room as it did occasionally during solemn moments, so the laugh sounded like a scream. Vivian caught her mother's angry glare.

The woman seemed not to notice. She touched Vivian's arm as she said in a loud whisper, "Did Grace tell you about the rose petals?"

"Grandmother told me nothing about Grace," Vivian said.

"Well, my, but we used to steal roses from Mr. and Mrs. Blake's yard and crush the petals." She winked. "Yes, we crushed them and folded them into our linens. Our clothes smelled nice, but I don't suppose it really did much good against the fish!" Her eyes clouded for a moment. "Fish are terribly domineering. Oh, they're quiet, little things all right, but they have the eyes of a mesmerizer."

Vivian smiled. "I knew Grandmother liked fish."

"Strange creatures," the woman sighed. Then, with a little gasp, she seemed to return to the present. "Well, child, we may not have smelled like roses, but some of us had poetic souls. Loretta, for one. Some of her poems appeared in the *Waxwood Review*." The clouds returned. "She died of puerile fever, poor thing, not long after Grace left."

"What sort of poetic soul did Grace have?" Vivian asked.

"You ought not to call her that, Viv." Jake murmured.

Vivian glared at him, then returned to Bertha. "I can't imagine Grandmother writing poetry."

"Oh, no!" The thought seemed to disturb the woman. "Grace's soul was too restless for that. Goodness, what would anyone with an adventurous spirit such as hers want with contemplative words?"

Vivian stared at a velvet pillow lying next to Ruth. Lines as long as cat scratches disturbed its smooth surface. She remembered Grandmother always sat there when people came to call, and, as she chatted pleasantly with the ladies, her nails raked the pillow as if the women's talk grated on her nerves. Vivian snatched it up and put it face down on her lap.

"I must see to my grandfather," Jake murmured as he bowed and left.

Bertha's eyes sparkled. "My, but you're a bright young lady. It isn't good for a woman whose soul is restless to be so bright. Especially when she's a belle."

"Am I a belle?" Vivian echoed. "I never thought about it before."

Bertha smiled. "I knew right away. I was a belle too, though you might not think it to look at me now." She glanced down at her shabby dress. "But, oh, I was a belle. Not bright and restless like you and Grace, though."

"If Grandmother didn't write poetry," Vivian prompted, "Where was her restless soul, then?"

The woman peered at her. "Why, on her drawing, naturally."

Vivian's eyes swept around the room, looking for Jake. He was coveted in a corner, bent over a handkerchief with a piece of chalk. Later, he would present her with a cheerful scene of a forest or a lily pond smeared in white powder on the black linen.

She sighed. "I should have realized. She taught my brother to draw."

"Fish!"

The word shot out above the hushed murmur. Vivian was thankful her mother was preoccupied with a burly man at the other end of the room.

Bertha lowered her voice. "Grace used to call them her little Tiresias. She could draw fish! Every gill, every fin, and those eyes — mercy!"

Vivian thought of Grandmother silent and attentive at social gatherings where Washington Street blue bloods had shown off their art collections. She would watch Grandmother examine the paintings and sculptures and wonder about the glint in her eye that spoke of both envy and rapture.

"I wonder why she stopped," she murmured.

"Stopped? Oh, dear!" Bertha's eyes widened.

"She taught Jake to draw, but she never drew herself," Vivian continued. "Not that we knew of, anyway."

"Perhaps she stopped because Mr. Alderdice didn't like it," Ruth piped up.

Vivian glanced at her. "Mr. Alderdice?"

"Your grandfather."

Vivian remembered Grandfather watching Grandmother in this very same room where her portrait looked upon them with its gracious countenance. He would hold his pipe to his lips without lighting it and observe as she worked on her embroidery or read a book or stared into the fire with her chin in her hand. He would hardly speak a word to her all evening, preferring to chatter with Larissa instead, and yet he would watch Grandmother, as if trying to pry open her mind.

"Oh, but he liked it, mercy, he did," Bertha lamented. "He liked her fish."

Something about the way the woman was looking at Vivian made her feel uneasy. "Grandmother had other duties," she said. "It would have been odd for her to have taken up drawing. And maybe a little scandalous."

"Oh, heavens, Grace wouldn't have cared about *that*," Bertha said. "She didn't care what people thought. At least she didn't when she went away with *him*."

"Him?"

"Evan." She glanced up at Vivian. "To Brandywine. Why, didn't you know, child?"

"Mother, you're talking too much," Ruth snapped.

The elderly woman looked down into the sherry glass, still untouched. A seething silence filled the room.

Grandfather appeared just then, looming like a statue of Zeus. Vivian rose and took his arm. "We've been having a lovely chat about Grandmother." She peered at his perplexed face.

"Waxwood?" The daze softened his face for a moment.

"Yes, Grandfather," she said. "Bertha's been telling me all about Waxwood."

"You remember, Malcolm," the woman said. "Oh, heavens, you *must* remember."

A thundering countenance glared back at her. "You shall not put Norma on the pyre of love!" he declared. "Get out, Adalgisa, get out!"

"Grandfather!" Vivian clutched his hand.

"Norma." Bertha's eyes rolled. "The opera in the city park that summer, oh, yes, what a treat!"

"Her pyre is mine!" His finger pointed at the windows. "Our love is holier and everlasting love and shall begin—" He collapsed almost in Vivian's arms.

Larissa rushed forward with the two footmen, the burly man trailing behind them. Vivian recognized him as one of the foremen at Alderdice Shipping. "Father." Her mother took over with a gentle command. "Let us take you upstairs now."

He stared at his daughter's face like a bewildered child. "Risa, my darling Risa." He touched her face. "More Alderdice than I."

"Yes, Father."

Just as the footmen took hold of his arms, Jake pulled his grandfather out of their grasp, his face melted with compassion. Her mother's eyes were damp, and she said nothing as Jake led Grandfather out of the parlor.

Mrs. Bilton and a few of the auxiliary ladies herded the last of the mourners out the door, casting compassionate glances at Larissa as they did so. In a few moments, everyone but the Rosses were gone.

Larissa turned to Bertha. "You see now why I asked you not to come. You've disturbed my father terribly."

Ruth held tight to her mother's chair. "It was your daughter who invited us to stay, Mrs. Alderdice. Remember?"

"But I said nothing, nothing!" Bertha screeched. "He was the one who reminded me of *Norma*!"

"Have you no respect for our bereavement?" Larissa continued in a rasping voice.

"Ruth is right, Mother," Vivian said. "It's my fault Grandfather's upset."

Larissa shot her a look of silence. "I must ask you to leave. Now."

"Oh, no!" Bertha squeaked. "This young woman has been such pleasant company, is it a sin to find pleasant company at such an occasion? It isn't a sin, is it?" She clawed Vivian's hand.

"Whether or not it's a sin, madam, is hardly the point," said the burly man. "It ain't proper for you to stay."

"You have no business saying such a thing considering you're not a part of it!" Vivian snapped.

"Mr. Flagg is more a part of this family than Mrs. and Miss Ross." Larissa's tone sharpened like a knife. "He's known your grandfather since he was a young man."

The man bowed in gratitude.

"And I knew Grace when she was a debutante!" Bertha shrieked.

Jake returned and whispered to Vivian, "I gave Grandfather his sleeping powders."

Larissa looked at her squarely. "I don't believe you ever knew my mother, Mrs.Ross."

"Mother!"

"You've been taking advantage of my daughter's kindness and our misfortune."

Bertha dropped the tiny glass. The sherry made a small spot on the carpet.

"You've no call to say such a thing." Ruth's gaze narrowed.

"How can you be so ungracious?" Vivian's eyes were damp.

"On the contrary," said her mother. "We've been most gracious. But upsetting an old man already devastated by his wife's death is beyond endurance."

"I knew Grace. I knew her!" the woman squeaked.

Vivian put her hand around the small shoulders. "Of course you did, Bertha. You paid your respects just like everyone else."

Ruth eyed Larissa. "Why don't you ask your daughter why she was asking so many questions about her grandmother, Mrs. Alderdice?"

"I didn't say a word about Evan." Bertha's finger pointed in a vague direction. "She asked me, but I didn't say a word."

"We know no Evan," Larissa said. Bertha let out a cry. "I'm sorry if I've alarmed you, but you must understand this is a very trying time for us." Her tone softened. "Mr. Flagg will see you reach home safely." The man stepped forward.

"I've said nothing," Bertha whispered. "Nothing."

"At least we can feed these good women, Mother." Vivian took Jake's arm. Her eyes fell on the spilled sherry. It suddenly came to her why Bertha hadn't touched it. "Drinking makes one dizzy if one hasn't eaten in a while, doesn't it?"

Ruth's cheeks turned scarlet. "We came to offer our condolences. We've done so, and now the time has come for us to leave."

"We were young women together." Bertha's voice was almost a hoarse whisper. "Why, we went to the same parties, saw the same beaus, and once, once, she gave me a present for my birthday. She drew a mermaid." She met Jake's eyes with a wild look. "I still have the picture. Mercy, why didn't I bring it?"

"Please, Mama," her daughter begged. "Come, we'll go home now."

Bertha's strength deflated, and she slumped down, her hands tumbling in her lap as her daughter pushed the rolling chair out of the room. Vivian leapt forward, pulling away from Jake's attempt to hold her back. She reached the doorway, seeing only an empty hallway. As she came back into the room, she heard her mother say, "She knows nothing. *Nothing.*"

CHAPTER 4

$\mathcal{T}$hough the parlor was now empty, Vivian still felt smothered by the velvet drapes and covered mirrors. "Mother," she ventured, "may I open just one window? Please?"

"Absolutely not!" Larissa shot her a look.

"But it's stifling!"

"Your improprieties have reached the limit, Vivian." She glanced at the servants whom Basset had ushered to clear the glasses and dust the room. "I'm going to see to your grandfather."

"I'll go with you." Jake stepped forward.

"I would rather go alone."

"Jake is as concerned about Grandfather as the rest of us, Mother." Vivian recalled his grave face earlier.

"I never said he wasn't." Larissa cleared her throat. "I shall be back shortly."

Vivian sprang forward, taking her mother's hand. "Mother, let us talk first, and then we can all go. The three of us."

"We'll talk when I return." Her mother slipped her hand out of her grasp. "Jacob, you may go to bed."

After her mother left, the stifling feeling increased, making Vivian hot and damp in the heavy black dress. She took her brother's hand and squeezed it. "She oughtn't to behave so horribly toward us."

"You pushed her too far today," her brother mumbled.

Vivian looked at him, amused. "Isn't that what a Dagger Girl does?"

His lips creased into something like a grim smile. "She hasn't called you that in ages."

"One never lets go of a dagger, dear."

He slid into the tête-à-tête. "Do you really think it's true?"

"What's true?"

"What that woman said?"

She stared at the cushion. It seemed almost tainted now with visions of her grandmother's raking fingernails. "We should put this in the attic," she remarked.

He repeated, "Do you think that woman really knew Grandmother?"

She saw Bertha Ross's dancing eyes and felt the leathery hands shaking as they held the delicate sherry glass. "Of course she did."

She could see how frightened he was by the way his hands pressed into his knees.

Vivian sat down beside him and studied her grandmother's well-sculpted face. "I admired this painting once."

"I remember how glad Grandfather was when they brought it from Great-Grandfather's house."

Vivian glanced at him. "You must have been three or four."

The boyish features, so unlike the Alderdice angularity, became boorish. "You don't think I would remember Grandfather laughing? He laughed, you know. He was so proud, he laughed."

"He hardly ever laughs now," Vivian murmured.

He looked hard at her. "You don't admire the portrait anymore?"

"It reminds me of the marionette show we saw in Lafayette

Park last year." The show had featured a doll named Annabella with rosy cheeks, stunned eyes, and a butterfly mouth who moved to suit her master's fancy. Grandmother's vacant, lovely features looked up at her from the painting just like Annabella's.

"It's because she isn't smiling," her brother lamented. "She ought to be smiling."

Vivian realized for the first time how the melancholy day had left him unhinged. "Do what Mother says, dear," she said gently. "Go to bed."

His eyes blinked at the portrait. "I wish she were smiling."

She stiffened. "Would it make Bertha's words go away if she were?"

"That woman was confused, Viv."

"Under how many layers of confusion is the truth hidden?" she asked.

"Put it away and don't think any more about it." He put his arm around her shoulder. "Isn't that what Mother is always telling us?"

The eyes in the portrait reminded her of glass, shiny and one-dimensional. "It was her coming out picture. Perhaps that's why she isn't smiling."

"I thought all debutantes were exuberant at their coming out."

"No," Vivian said in a quiet voice. "Not all."

He rose and began to pace, pounding one hand into the other.

"She probably never really posed for it," said Vivian. "In fact, I'm certain of it. I remember now. Mother showed me a picture of Grandmother as a debutante. It was the same pink dress and pearls. The same pose."

"You make it sound so horrible."

"Not horrible," Vivian said. "Unreal. Something unreal in her face, like a phantom." She turned to her brother. "I'm beginning to believe grandmother's life was filled with illusions."

"What sort of illusions?"

"I don't know," she said. "I only feel she buried her Unmentionables well before we buried her. Artless in her very art of angelic repose."

They sat in silence on the *tête-à-tête together* in silence as the servants collected the rest of the sherry glasses.

Soon Larissa reappeared, looking tranquil and contained. Her face hid the precious grief that had previously softened its contours. As she stared at the portrait, the hard shell of her face cracked, and a little twitch began at the corner of her mouth.

"Are you all right, Mother?" Vivian held out her hand.

The strange expression disappeared. Her elongated face showed the elegance and control that always awed the women of Washington Street. "She was always trying to give those pearls away. She thought they didn't suit her."

"They don't suit her," Vivian agreed. "Pink hardly becomes a strawberry blond."

"Nonsense. Nothing could be lovelier," her mother insisted.

"Pale hides pale," Jake pointed out.

She gave him a sharp look. "I thought I told you to go to bed."

"Please, Mother, don't be hard on him," Vivian murmured. "Not now when our mourning is just beginning."

Jake rose. "Shall I be like Grandfather and take a sleeping powder?"

"How dare you speak of your grandfather like that!" Her mother looked horrified. "I told you to go to bed, Jacob."

But in one of his rare flashes of obstinacy, he sat back with his hands folded.

Larissa turned her back on him and gripped Vivian's arm. "And now for *you*, young lady. You wanted to talk and we shall talk."

"Yes," Vivian said. "About Waxwood and about Evan."

Larissa's blue eyes grew opaque.

"Evan," Vivian repeated. "That name disturbed Mrs. Ross very much."

"Yes, well, it's about *that woman* I want to talk to you." Larissa motioned her toward one of the overstuffed chairs.

"I don't want to sit down!"

"Vivian." Her mother's voice dimmed. "Don't be trying. Not today, not now."

Her mother's shoulders sagged, her face lined deeper than her thirty-seven years. Vivian slid on the couch and took her hand.

Larissa patted her head. "You've always done what I've asked, dear. But lately, you've been forgetting your position."

"My position?"

"You're the granddaughter of Malcolm Alderdice," her mother said in a firm voice. "That means something in San Francisco."

"I was the granddaughter of Penelope Alderdice too," Vivian said. "Doesn't that mean something?"

"I don't quite know what you mean."

"A door has opened," Vivian murmured.

"One need not walk through every open door." Larissa gave her a meaningful look. "Especially if a madwoman holds the key."

"Mrs. Ross isn't mad," Jake ventured. "Confused, but not mad."

His mother gave him a look. She continued in a rasping voice. "Your behavior today was abominable. I trust I needn't remind you how necessary it is to conduct oneself honorably during times like these."

"No, Mother," Vivian breathed. "You needn't remind me."

Her mother's tone became sorrowful. "I realize this is all very troubling."

Vivian said with a grimace. "Troubling is hardly the word."

"Don't be ironic!"

Vivian eyed her. "I wouldn't dream of it."

"You deliberately disobeyed me and invited Mrs. Ross and her daughter. That woman's mad declarations put your grandfather in a terrible state."

"Even in oblivion, one may understand the secrets of a dead soul," Jake murmured.

Larissa's voice rose. "Don't you start!"

"You insist Bertha Ross is mad but, as Jake said, she isn't. And you know it, don't you, Mother?" Her mother was silent. "Don't you?"

Larissa removed the veil thrown back over her head. "I don't say she didn't know your grandmother for certain."

"You no longer deny it?"

"She *might* have."

"Because Grandmother lived in Waxwood?"

"She did not *live* in Waxwood," her mother said archly. "She went there for a visit one summer."

"When?"

"Vivian, you're being too inquisitive." Larissa brushed her hand against her forehead.

"If it was only a visit, why were you so frightened when you saw Bertha in the chapel?" Vivian leaned forward. "And why was Grandfather so distraught when he saw her?"

"I was irritated," her mother insisted. "And your grandfather was distraught because his wife has just died."

"He's been terribly distressed since he found Grandmother," Jake ventured.

Vivian said, "He's been lost, not distressed."

"He's not been himself—" Jake lamented.

"He's in a daze!" Vivian insisted. "His mind is slowly dissipating."

Her mother bit her lip. "Must you always twist the dagger, Vivian?"

"Dagger Girl," Jake mumbled.

"Jacob, I told you to go to bed!"

The hostile tone roused Jake from his laconic mood. With his hands in the pockets of his mourning jacket, he stalked out of the room.

Vivian gripped the back of her mother's chair. "I wish you would try to understand, Mother."

"Understand?"

"We're both upset because we've just discovered our grandmother is not the woman we thought we knew but someone else."

"She shouldn't have stayed," said Larissa. "She shouldn't have told you those things."

"Before you said she oughtn't to have come. Now you say she shouldn't have stayed." Vivian eyed her. "You expected her to come, even after you sent her the note, didn't you?"

"You read too much into things, Vivian," said Larissa. "They knew someone named Grace, not Penelope Alderdice."

"You admit Bertha could have known Grandmother the summer she stayed in Waxwood."

Her mother clasped her hands together. "Waxwood is a tiny town. She may have crossed this woman's path. I meant nothing more."

"Bertha said they were friends."

"Your grandmother was raised in San Francisco!" Her mother took her hands. "She lived here all her life. She loved the city."

"Grandfather knows," Vivian said. "I saw his face when he looked at Bertha. He knows."

"He knew they were imposters and that unsettled him, dear."

"I don't think that's true, and I don't think you believe it's true either."

Larissa looked alarmed for a moment, and her eyes snapped to the portrait. "I remember how three women came to my grandmother's funeral, all in exactly the same dress. They were so decrepit, they could barely walk. They *insisted* they had gone to school with Grandmother."

Vivian blinked. "But they hadn't?"

"Your grandmother was educated at home by a governess like any respectable girl of her time," Larissa sniffed. "They read of your great-grandmother's death in the newspaper and believed whole-heartedly she was their dear friend."

"Why would they do such a thing?"

Her mother shrugged. "Perhaps they wanted to reassure themselves of their own immortality, or perhaps they were mad like Mrs. Ross."

"Then why was Grandfather so frightened?"

"He was not frightened!" Her mother growled. "It's all been too much for him. He's not a young man, Vivian."

"Did you know Grandmother was an artist?"

Larissa smiled a little. "She dabbled with paints just like most young women did back then."

"She drew fish." Vivian rattled. "A rather odd subject for a dabbler to choose."

"Your grandmother had some strange ideas when she was young." That same twitch returned to the corner of her mouth, but only for a moment. "Many young women have silly notions but they leave them behind when they marry."

"Or someone like Grandfather forces them to leave them behind," Vivian mumbled.

"He rather liked her drawings." Her mother cocked her head.

"That's exactly what Mrs. Ross said!" Vivian stared at her.

"She chose to give it up," Larissa continued. "After I was born, she burned all her sketchbooks." She covered her forehead with her hand. "Come, dear, it's been a long day."

Vivian looked at her with pleading eyes. "Mother, please tell me who Evan was."

"I haven't the faintest idea." Larissa did not look at her. "Probably some man Mrs. Ross knew in her youth."

"Then he might have known Grandmother."

"More likely he was an apparition of that woman's mind." Larissa pressed her hands against her forehead again. "What does it matter?"

"I don't know," Vivian said. "I don't know yet."

"It has nothing to do with us." Her mother rose. "Come, dear, it's time we went to bed."

As they climbed the stairs, Larissa gripped her hand. "Vivian, promise me you won't speak of this again. You won't even think about it again."

Vivian looked at her mother's gaunt face as it caught the shadows of light, the hollows around her eyes outlined. She recalled her brother's words: *Put it away and don't think about it. Isn't that what Mother is always telling us?* "I'll try, Mother." She felt suddenly tired.

She put her arm around her. "Mrs. Ross and her apparitions will fade away. You'll see."

Vivian gazed at the archway above the stairs. Mrs. Ross may have apparitions, as her mother said, and she may not. But she herself would not soon fade away in Vivian's mind.

CHAPTER 5

$\mathcal{F}$og penetrated the walls of Alderdice Hall during the night. Vivian shivered more from fear than cold as the smoke, seeing almost nothing but the gleam of the candle by her bedside in the early morning darkness. She sat up in bed, her arms and legs stiff and her spine aching. She thought of Ancestor Hall, that marble room reserved for the paintings of Alderdice ancestors. Grandfather insisted on capturing those buried ghosts for future generations to ponder. Her grandmother's portrait would soon take its place among them.

She reached under her pillow for Bertha's letter. She had reread it at least a dozen times since last night. The voice of the elderly woman leapt from every word, confused and yet coherent. Though she promised her mother last night, she knew she couldn't remain ignorant about the woman her grandmother had been, even if only for a summer. It intruded her dreams the entire night, permeable as a ghost, the specter reaching out its arms to her, pulling her after it.

It was still dim outside when she slipped out of her room. She peeked through the crack of Jake's bedroom door. He gave her a wrinkled smile and set aside the sketchbook. "I've come to take you on a picnic," she announced.

"You're mad!"

"Not mad, Jake. Curious. Mother would say that's worse than mad, wouldn't she?" she asked ruefully.

His head sunk back against the pillow. "What are you curious about?"

She studied him. "The specter that's just appeared in our lives."

He sniffed. "You mean Bertha Ross?"

"I mean our own grandmother."

"And you think Bertha Ross is going to exorcise it for you?"

"Not just me, Jake." She leaned against the bedpost. "Us." At the confusion on his face, she said, "I'm going to Waxwood to take Bertha and Ruth out for a picnic because she knows things about Grandmother that Mother won't tell us." She eyed him. "I want you to come with me."

"You *are* mad." His face paled.

"I believe Bertha was telling the truth, Jake."

"The truth about what?"

"Grandmother *did* go to Waxwood," she said. "And she *did* know Bertha Ross."

"What if she did?"

"It wouldn't surprise me if Grandmother had some adventure there she doesn't want us to know about." She paced the narrow room. "It occurred to me yesterday that Grandmother taught you to draw not only because she saw you had talent. She was trying to relive some past experience through you. Happier times, perhaps."

"People do foolish things when they're young," he lamented.

"And what foolish things will you do when Grandfather dies and you inherit everything?" She challenged him.

"That won't happen for a long time," he said in a rough tone.

Vivian fingered the teddy bear on the bureau. "We used to

laugh about the Unmentionables, Jake. Those things we knew existed but no one talked about. It's no longer a laughing matter."

"Every family has something to hide," he pointed out.

"There is a difference between hiding something and locking it away so as not to face it," she said.

He fidgeted with his drawing tools. "They're locked away because they don't matter."

"What does, then?" She cried. "The name of Alderdice because it 'means something' in San Francisco?"

"Maybe that's all that need matter to us," he said quietly.

"But it isn't, is it?" There was silence as the wind blew against the window pain. "Is it?" She repeated in a more forceful tone.

He sighed. "No, I suppose it isn't?"

She took his hand. "What if those heroic stories we were told about the Alderdices weren't so heroic? What if they're really an illusion?"

He looked at her with sad eyes. "I haven't your courage to twist the dagger, Viv."

"I"m not asking you to," she snapped. "I'm only asking you to be there with me."

He leaned his forehead against his knees.

She put her arms around him. "I'm tired of cowardice. Tired of sugar-water in my veins. I thought you were too."

He remained silent.

"If you won't go with me to Waxwood, I'll go alone."

His gaze was distant. "You know what Mother will do if she finds out what we've done."

She could barely hide her joy at the word "we"."I've no fear of Mother."

"And Grandfather?"

"I don't think either of us need to fear Grandfather any longer. Do you?"

He flinched as he pulled back the covers. "Sometimes you hurt others with your daggar-twisting, Viv."

She grabbed his hand. "It wasn't my dagger-twisting that brought Bertha Ross here yesterday."

"How can an old woman whose fancy is more vivid than her memory help us?"

"I don't know." Vivian dropped his hand. "But we must find out."

He was silent again, staring at the teddy bear she had abandoned. "I'm afraid, Viv."

She put her arms around him. "The truth can't hurt us, Jake."

He looked at her again with sad eyes. "It can when the truth lies in another person's dark room. Don't walk into other people's dark rooms, Viv."

She gave him a fierce look in spite of the mounting terror in her chest. "You'd better get dressed if you're coming with me."

He stared down at his hands, then nodded.

~~~~~

The first thing Vivian heard when they reached the train station was the strange tune of violins. The music eased Jake's tight features and made him look fifteen again. The agent stared at their mourning attire, uncertain and uncomfortable.

Vivian hesitated a moment before asking, "Which train stops at Waxwood?"

The man looked neither surprised nor curious. "That would be the Bowline Express to Monterey, miss. The 8:15."

"Can you get us tickets, please?" She asked

As they waited, the music bloomed into a full-blown opera tune with flutes and piccolos accompanying the violins.

"*Rigoletto*," Jake murmured.

The agent returned, clearly embarrassed. "I'm sorry, miss, but the parlor car is filled up. What with the opera company—"

"Are they playing the music?" Jake asked

The agent nodded. "That's from Mr. Ollerton's pupils, sir," he said. "The gentleman who owns the music school down on Pine Street."

"Yes, I know it," Jake said softly.

"A lively man, I daresay, but lets his pupils run a bit wild, if you know what I mean," the agent added.

"We must get on that train," Vivian said. "A friend of our grandmother's is very ill." She ignored her brother's sharp gaze.

"I could get you a seat on the 12:10," the man offered.

"No, no, that won't do." She was aware of the picnic basket on the ground behind her.

"If there's no train, Viv—" Jake began.

"What about the coach car?"

The man looked horrified. "The coach, miss?"

"Why not?"

The agent's eyes slid from one to the other, examining their mourning grab.

She sighed. "All right. The 12:10 it must be."

"Viv—"

"The 12:10," she said firmly.

When the agent had gone to get the ticket, she took Jake's arm and they wandered down the platform. Crowds formed near the tracks for the Bowline Express. They threaded their way around full-skirted women and bespectacled men.

"What is someone should see us?" Jake's nervous tone rose above the train noises.

"Why, Vivian!"

The jovial voice rose above the violins, making Vivian shrink back. But when a crowd of young women moved away, she saw it was Melvina Moore.

"You look as if you're about to throw yourself under the train," the woman continued. "Hello, Jacob."

He gave her a jerky bow.

"Come, you mustn't be another Anna Karenina." She took Vivian's arm, leading her to a bench. Jake followed with a slow stride.

"Are you taking the Bowline Express?" Vivian asked, glancing at her brother.

"Are you?" The woman's pert eyes regarded them both with amusement.

She glanced at the iron beast. "There's no more room in the parlor car, and the station agent insists it's unsuitable for us to take the passenger coach." Her hands went to the black skirt, wanting to yank it off.

"He's right," said the woman. "Come, I'll get you on that train."

She disappeared into the thick crowd. The violins began again.

Mrs. Moore returned. "We must hurry." She dragged Vivian and Jake to a front car and nearly lifted them onto it while a gentleman gazed at her, aghast. She gave him a knowing look in return as she boarded the train.

Vivian felt immediately reassured. "Thank you. We had to catch *this* train." She gave her brother a meaningful look.

Jake glanced around, pressing his hands together.

"This is a friend's private car," Marvina rcplsinrf. "He lets me borrow it sometimes." With a sly look, she added, "Your mother, I daresay, wouldn't approve."

"Mother has the utmost respect for you, Mrs. Moore," Jake said.

Vivian hid a smile, as she had heard Larissa and other Washington Street ladies refer to the widow as "an unfortunate resident this side of Nob Hill" because she preferred to remain a widow rather than remarry. Those with a more vicious tongue called her a bluestocking.

"You're a sweet, well-mannered young man, Jacob," Mrs. Moore said as she settled into the velvet seat. "Your mother had taught you well."

"She didn't teach us," Vivian said. "Our grandmother did."

The woman sighed. "I was sorry to hear of her death."

The sting of tears came to Vivian's eyes. Jake looked away.

Vivian spoke in a steady voice. "Grandmother was ill for quite some time, you know."

"You had time to prepare, then. An instant death — well, there's nothing more tragic, is there? Believe me, I know." A pained look appeared on her face, and Vivian wondered if she was thinking of her deceased husband.

"Yes, we were prepared," Vivian said softly. She sat down next to Jake, who was turned toward the window, his face nearly pressed against it.

Mrs. Moore reached into her small bag and produced two books. "Don't know why I bring the damn things when all I want to do is talk." She tossed them on the empty seat beside her. "If you don't mind my asking, why did you *have* to get on this train?"

Vivian blinked.

"You said you absolutely had to get on this train," the woman repeated. "You were quite Anna Kareninaish about it."

"I've never read *Anna Karenina*," Vivian mumbled.

"Good," Mrs. Moore declared. "Don't ever read it."

Vivian stared. "I thought you believed in women's education."

"I do, but it's such a tragic story." The woman sighed. "Even if Anna is a deplorable person when one comes right down to it."

Loud voices flew in through the open window. Vivian glanced at the platform. The conductor herded the young musicians into their seats with sharp reprimands. They ignored him, chattering and tuning their instruments.

"We had to get on this train because our grandmother's friend is ill," she said. "We want to see her."

She saw Jake flinch, but the white lie did not seem such a lie. Bertha Ross' behavior at the funeral had hardly been one of a woman in fine health.

"Is she in Monterey?" Mrs. Moore asked.

"Waxwood."

"How odd Penelope should have had a friend there."

Vivian sat forward. "Do you know it?" Jake's hand reached for hers, squeezing it with warning, but she paid no attention.

"I visited once," she admitted. "Not much to recommend it, I'm afraid. A little pier, no, two little piers. A shadow of a bay. And those strange trees."

"The waxwood trees?"

"Yes." Mrs. Moore glanced out the window. "I believe someone once called them an outlandish phenomenon. You ought to see them."

"Perhaps we will one day," Vivian murmured.

"They say some financiers are planning to open resorts there soon. It won't compare to San Francisco, but then, San Francisco is the jewel of the Pacific Coast, is it not?" She gave Jake a hearty wink.

"Yes, ma'am," he said politely.

Vivian sat back. "You make Waxwood sound rather dismal."

"I wouldn't say that. They have an art colony in the hills near the wax wood forest." She glanced at Jake. "That ought to interest you. You're an artist, aren't you, Jake?"

"I draw," he mumbled.

"Unfortunately, I'm told they're not very welcoming to visitors," the woman went on. "There is a little shop at the gate with some of the artists' work, though. Most charming."

"Do you know the name of it?" Vivian asked.

"Brandywine, I think."

The name caught Vivian's attention. She glanced at her brother, but his face remained stoic. "Our grandmother's friend mentioned that name."

Mrs. Moore chuckled. "They hardly seemed to have enough water, much less brandy or wine." She sighed. "Do either of you mind if I doze a bit?"

"Not at all," Vivian said and Jake nodded.

Vivian tried to form a picture of Waxwood in her mind, but all she could see were a blur of dark water and hills. The train jolted between valleys of goldenrod and green hills. There was still not much sun, and the sky was pale, but she felt no gloom. Strains of violins floated through the window as the young musicians picked up their tune again.

"*Carmen*," Jake mumbled.

"I wish they would stop that noise," Mrs. Moore said.

"Toreador's song," Vivian murmured.

The woman looked surprised. "You know the opera?"

"Doesn't that suit your idea of the educated woman?" Vivian couldn't help but smile.

"It seems the least likely thing to interest someone such as yourself." Mrs. Moore laughed.

"Jake knows it better than I do," Vivian admitted. "The extent of my knowledge is from a music box I received as one of my coming out gifts."

"I wouldn't think young ladies these days receive such refined gifts, nor appreciate them," Mrs. Moore laughed.

"My sister isn't like other young ladies," Jake said.

The woman smiled. "You're right, of course. I never thought you one of these frivolous girls, Vivian."

"What did you think of me, Mrs. Moore?" Vivian asked. "I really would like to know."

"Oh, quieter than most," she said. "I even thought you a little too sedate for my taste. But you're nothing of the kind, are you?" She gave her an even look.

Vivian's stomach tightened as if with the crescendo of the strings in the next car. "I don't know what I am yet."

Mrs. Moore patted her hand. "Tell me about the music box. I'm intrigued now."

Vivian smiled. "Grandfather gave it to me. You know my grandfather."

Mrs. Moore raised her eyebrows. "I imagine it's a massive thing of walnut and satinwood."

"With majestic gold handles," Vivian laughed. "It looks like an enormous lap dog. Jake calls it Cerberus."

"Hades' three-headed watchdog," he explained without looking away from the window.

Mrs. Moore nodded. "How delightful."

"The music from it is grand, though." Vivian sighed. "It's what rain would sound like if rain could speak."

"Charming way of putting it," the woman murmured. "And it plays opera tunes?"

"*Carmen*, of course. *Rigoletto*. And Bellini." The last fell like a nail on a wooden floor.

"You mean Bellini's *Norma*?"

Vivian nodded, playing with her gloves.

"I saw it once in Madrid. Terribly tragic." Mrs. Moore was silent for a moment. "Not a very popular opera. But I'd like to hear some of the songs from *Norma* one day."

"I'm afraid I haven't got the music box anymore," Vivian said quickly. "I gave it away." She felt her brother's stare on her but when she turned her head, his gaze had gone back to the window.

"A pity." Mrs. Moore leaned back and closed her eyes. The tone of her voice made Vivian realize she didn't believe her but she was too discreet to ask more questions.

"You'd better get some rest, Viv," Jake said, his tone sounding older than fifteen. "We've a ways to go yet."

Behind closed eyes, Vivian saw Grandmother as she used to be, her sedate features in repose. Grandmother leaning back as Vivian opened the music box, a gray shade overriding her blue eyes, and her head bobbing back and forth to the chimes of the tune.

"Do you know it, Grandmother?" Vivian had asked.

Her grandfather was the one who answered. "From *Norma*."

"Father?" Larissa looked up from her embroidery.

"'Casta Diva,'" he went on.

Her mother sighed. "We must take Vivian to the opera now that she's nearly of age."

A frightened look appeared on Grandmother's face. "Not that one, surely!"

Jake, who had been drawing on a piece of folded paper, held the pencil in his hand as if ready to stab someone. His fourteen-year-old boyish face became as wrinkled as an eighty-year-old man's.

Larissa remained impassive as she examined the embroidered silk. "Dorothy was telling me just the other day about a revival of *The Gypsy Baron*. They went last week and found it rather amusing."

"Strauss always is," Grandfather chimed in.

"We might go next week—"

Grandfather's eyebrows puckered, and his cheeks drew firm. He watched Grandmother as her fingers dug into the folds of her evening dress. Her head rolled from one side to the other. He rose and, without his walking stick, strolled over to the *tête-à-tête*. He bent down and plucked the pillow from her lap, tossing it on the empty seat. Grandmother's head was still, her hands folded neatly in her lap.

Larissa rose and slid the cushion behind her mother's back. "That's better, isn't it, Mother?"

Grandmother asked sharply, "Is it?"

Grandfather looked out the window at the starry night. "Play that tune again," he ordered.

Vivian hardly realized he was speaking to her. He did not turn to look at her. Her mother once insisted Grandfather did not mean to be curt, but he had been working since he was a young man and learned to get on with the matter at hand as quickly as possible. But that night, he spoke slowly, his voice seeping into the room.

"Your grandfather likes that tune, Vivian," her mother said.

"Grandmother doesn't." She tried to catch her eye. "You don't, do you?"

Her grandmother lowered her eyes, staring at the rose on the carpet, "the bleeding rose," Jake called it. Something had gone awry with the pattern, and the petals flopped every which way.

"Play it!" Grandfather's voice was more commanding.

Vivian lay her hands on top of the music box, feeling its smooth surface masking the vibrancy of the music.

"Play it!"

She turned the key, and the tune began. But the music no longer sounded like raindrops on glass.

The train made Vivian jump. Mrs. Moore was asleep. The music from the coach car had ceased.

Beside her, she heard her brother whisper, "Where is the music box, Viv?"

Vivian crossed to the other side of the car and opened the window all the way. Even the breeze could not lift the weighty melancholy that had overtaken her.

She had not given the music box away. After that evening, she had buried it behind the wooden cupboard in the playroom. She felt the music had been a warning of an agony too painful for her grandmother to remember but too compelling to forget.

CHAPTER 6

*I*t was early afternoon when they stepped off the train at the Waxwood station.

"It looks rather pitiful, doesn't it?" Jake remarked. The jerkiness in his voice and movements returned as he took the picnic basket from Vivian's arm.

Vivian could see what Mrs. Moore meant about "nothing there." Train tracks ran along a paltry bay and the hills beyond looked yellow and dry.

"Perhaps we should take the train back," he suggested.

A woman selling flowers passed by them. She didn't look at them but there was a smile on her face, as if she were smiling at the sun. All at once, Vivian felt at ease in this small village with its calm waters and neglected street.

She pulled Jake to the station window. The agent's expression seemed pastoral as he nodded at them from his caged window.

"We're looking for Mrs. Bertha Ross," she said.

"Well, now, Bertha's got that criss-cross house on the corner of Mueller Street," the man answered.

"Criss-cross house?"

"Go down here, make a right, and go up the hill a ways. Right there on the corner. Couldn't miss it, even if you only had one eye." He chuckled.

"May we leave this with you?" She took the heavy picnic basket from Jake.

"Ain't no ice box here," the agent cautioned.

"That's all right." Vivian said.

As they walked, her hand clutching Jake's arm, she absorbed the trance-like air of the town. Perhaps Grandmother had walked the same street, following it down to the bay, and then dipped their hands in the water. Perhaps she had even fished there.

"Remember when Grandmother told us how Great-Grandfather Merton used to take her down to wharf and let her sit on the dock and fish?" Vivian asked.

He shrugged. "What of it?"

"Maybe Grandmother fished on that pier too." Vivian threw her head toward the peek of bobbing wood that peered between an alley as they passed.

Two men passed, tipping their hats. Jake cautiously returned the sentiment.

People in the shops peered at them through the window. Vivian realized she looked a somber figure in her heavy black silk and beads. She imagined they were mumbling of how a lady in mourning oughtn't to be out on the street at this time of day, perhaps at all.

"What lengths must one go to exorcise a specter?" she mused.

"Stop saying that!" Jake burst out. "You make Grandmother sound like a ghost."

"Not Grandmother," she said. "Only the legacy she left."

They passed a charming park with wooly trees and a gazebo marked the edge of the road, breathing the sweet scent of spring. The tenseness in Jake's shoulders seemed to ease and Vivian heard him breath a sigh of relief.

They found the criss-cross house. The place was run-down

with faded gray and blue paint. Blue boards criss-crossed the gray walls, and the closed shutters had criss-cross boards as well.

The door flew open, and a foreboding figure darkened the entrance. She and Jake were both startled at the deep lines that made Ruth Ross's face stand out like a mask.

Vivian regained her composure first. "Good afternoon, Ruth. Do you remember us?"

The woman's eyes narrowed like an insect's. "I could hardly forget, could I?"

"Good afternoon, Miss Ross." Jake tipped his hat.

"What is it you want, Miss Alderdice?"

"Call us Vivian and Jake," Vivian said.

"My mother can be very careless about making acquaintances," she said curtly. "I am not."

Vivian tried not to flinch. Her brother had let go of her hand and was half-turned toward the street as if ready to leave at a moment's notice.

"We came to apologize." Vivian took the lead.

"For what?"

"Our mother's behavior toward you and Bertha," she said. "Even under the circumstances, it was inexcusable."

Ruth leaned against the doorframe. "Why is she not here herself to apologize?"

Vivian shifted. "Well, she's in mourning."

"So are you," Ruth pointed out.

"She sent us in her stead," Jake mumbled. But unlike Vivian, his lie came out sounding hollow.

"I see."

"We'd like to apologize in person to your mother, if we may." Vivian tried to sound brisk.

"I'm sorry, but I can't allow that."

"Please," she begged. "Mother really feels terrible about yesterday."

"I highly doubt that," Ruth said.

"Mother's been devastated by Grandmother's death," Vivian insisted. "She didn't grasp who your mother was or what she was doing there."

The woman leaned forward. "Did you, I wonder?"

"We shouldn't be here if we didn't." Vivian stiffened.

"I meant *you*, Miss Gossling." She glanced at Jake. "I've a feeling this was all your idea."

"I'm here willingly with my sister, Miss Ross." Jake's rough tone surprised even Vivian. "Our apology is sincere, whether you believe it or not."

The woman was silent for a moment. When she spoke, her voice was kinder. "I appreciate your good intentions but Mama is asleep."

"In the middle of the afternoon?" Vivian eyed the woman.

"She didn't sleep well last night," Ruth snapped. "Your mother wasn't the only one who was upset."

Jake looked at Vivian, his eyes showing capitulation as he took her hand and turned toward the gate.

Vivian wretched free and, climbing halfway up the steps, called out, "Bertha!"

She expected Ruth to slam the door. Instead, the woman gave her a sad look and motioned them inside.

Vivian's instincts had been right. Bertha was in the kitchen finishing her morning coffee, a small plate with crumbs in front of her, as if she had just finished breakfast. "Oh! I thought I heard someone calling me." The woman looked frightened for a moment.

Jake came forward and took her hand and kissed it. It was the right thing to do, as the woman's eyes brightened and she smiled with contentment.

"They've come to apologize for their mother, Mama." Ruth said.

The woman, so humble and grave in her chair, reminded Vivian of her grandmother. Something inside her crumbled, and she collapsed at the woman's feet, letting the tears come. These did not gather at the corners of her eyes but ran right down her cheeks onto her dress.

"There, there, child." Bertha patted her shoulders.

Vivian rose, staring out the kitchen window as she gathered her composure. Jake put his arm around her. Even the lines in Ruth's face disappeared.

"I'm sorry," she said. "I can't think what came over me."

"Grief is like that, oh, it just comes like a wave." Bertha sighed.

"Then we must erase it with happier times." Vivian smiled. "That's another reason why we came. We'd like to take you and Ruth on a picnic, if you'll come."

"Why, I haven't been on a picnic since Ruthie was a little girl." Bertha's eyes grew misty. "I could walk then. I could even run."

"I remember." Her daughter said in a soft voice.

"We went on so many picnics when we were belles. I could walk and run as well as any of them." Bertha chuckled. "Can you see me running up and down the pier in my stockings and singing with the gulls, Ruthie?"

For the first time, Ruth smiled. It was the heartening smile of a woman with great compassion. In the gleam of sunlight, she looked lovely.

"I can," Jake volunteered.

"Bless you, child." The woman pressed his hand.

"I shouldn't think a picnic were appropriate," Ruth murmured.

"Oh, but why not?" Bertha stared at her.

"Mama, really! They're in mourning."

The woman looked disturbed. "But they're so young. What a ghastly thought to be shut out from the sun because of that!"

"Ghastly or not, it's not proper," Ruth said sternly. "I think they ought to go home."

Jake inched toward his sister and whispered, "She's right, Viv. We ought to go home."

"But it's such a lovely day," Bertha insisted.

"Consider the picnic a gesture of friendship," Vivian said. "One wants one's friends about when one is in mourning."

"Yes, yes!" The elderly woman agreed.

"Let's be frank, Miss Alderdice." Ruth crossed her arms. "My mother and I feel no friendship toward you, and you and your brother feel none toward us."

"It takes time to be friends," Jake murmured.

"Grace was my friend, dear." Bertha's eyes filled with tears. "I see no reason her lovely granddaughter and grandson can't be ours too." She reached both her hands out, and Vivian and Jake graciously took them.

Her daughter sighed. "You're an innocent soul, Mama. You don't see."

"See?"

"They've come to accost you with questions."

"I have no questions," Jake growled.

"*You* don't," she said in a pointed tone. "But your sister does. Don't you, Miss Alderdice?"

Vivian's heart pounded. "I deserve that after what happened yesterday."

Ruth stiffened. "Have you given a thought to how unsettled *my* mother was after yesterday's events?"

"Oh, but I'm fine now, and an outing is just the thing. Grace always said, 'sunshine heals all malady.'" Bertha's eyes were bright.

"Don't you, Miss Alderdice?" Ruth repeated.

"Don't I what?"

"Have questions about your grandmother no one else will answer?"

"Questions no one else *can* answer." Vivian corrected.

"I'm sure they could if they chose to." Ruth's eyes were hard.

"We don't have questions," Jake insisted.

"Oh, questions, I don't mind questions," Bertha said.

"I know, Mama. You would just as soon talk about your girl-hood as breathe," said her daughter. "But some Pandora's boxes are best left locked."

"We have no Pandora's box —" Jake began, but looking at his sister's face, he fell silent.

"I'm sure you don't, Mr. Alderdice," said Ruth. "But your sister is a different matter."

Vivian was silent for a moment. "I've been uncertain about a lot of things since yesterday. I'm prepared to open my Pandora's box of woes."

"What good could it possibly do you?"

Vivian "looked at her squarely. "I believe there's a phantom in it."

"Viv!" Jake was genuinely alarmed. She felt his hand shaking in hers.

"We must release that phantom," Vivian continued, feeling less bold than she sounded. "Light erases a phantom, and I think your mother is that light."

"Mercy!" Bertha clasped the cross hanging around her throat.

"You see how you're alarming my mother?" Ruth petted the elderly woman's hand. "Now I *must* as you to leave."

"Ruthie!"

Vivian's eyes flashed. "Don't you think your mother may decide for herself?"

"My mother is in my care." Ruth's entire figure shook with rage.

Vivian pressed Bertha's hand, her eyes filling with tears. "Please help me."

The woman looked from her daughter to Vivian and Jake. Her chest heaved, and her eyes soften, collapsing the dancing light in them. When she spoke, she sounded assured for the first time. "One mustn't refuse to be a light, Ruthie."

Her daughter's expression softened. "You really want to go on this picnic, Mama?"

"We must have light," her mother repeated.

She looked at Vivian.' "All right. We'll go on your picnic."

Bertha bounced with joy. "We could sit on the pier! We could, couldn't we? Oh, we had such fun there once!"

"Whatever you wish, Mama." As Ruth hung the towel on the back of a chair, Vivian observed her hands were unsteady.

~~~~~

"Yes, sir, Grace made the best salmon cakes in the county!"

They sat on the pier. Bertha's chair was as close to the edge as Ruth would allow, a roast beef sandwich in her lap. Ruth filled a cup with cider from a jug she had brought along with her.

"She used to make them in our house all the time," Bertha continued, looking brightly at Jake. "Before she discovered her little Tiresias, that is."

"Grandmother making salmon cakes," Vivian mused. "I can hardly imagine it."

"I daresay," Ruth said with a smirk. "When one lives one's life entirely upstairs."

Jake stiffened. "Our grandmother led a lady's life."

"But she was spoiled, Jake," Vivian admitted.

"Spoiled, yes, she was spoiled," Bertha agreed. "Spoil is a literal word too, you know. What one never uses goes to rot, doesn't it?" Her eyes became fuzzy. "*We* never spoiled Grace. Oh, we had our cook and our maid, but she made salmon cakes and pies and lemonade. She enjoyed doing things for people."

"Yes, she did." Vivian thought of the poise woman in the parlor portrait.

"Why, I imagine she would have done all the cooking and sewing when she stayed with us. If Mama would have let her." The pealing laughter carried in the wind.

"I can see she was happy here." Vivian smiled.

"She was on vacation," Jake said in a low voice.

"It was more than that, dear boy." Bertha rocked back and forth. "She was free too, or so she said."

"Free?"

"I imagine she found her social obligations in the city rather constricting," Ruth remarked. "She was a debutante when she came, wasn't she, Mama?"

"We all were, dear," said Bertha. "We had our own society here in Waxwood and, oh, what fun we had!"

"But you said she came to Waxwood to get away from society," her daughter persisted.

"It was odd, so odd." Bertha looked puzzled. "That's what she said and yes, she enjoyed being with the belles and the beaus."

"You said my grandmother drew a mermaid for your birthday." Vivian leaned forward. "May I see it after lunch?"

"Viv —"

"I don't think you have it, do you, Mama?" Ruth asked.

"Oh, somewhere." Bertha looked at the bay. "How strange she was that night."

"What night?" Vivian asked.

"My twentieth birthday party. Why, certainly she was strange. Almost like Ebba."

"Who was Ebba?"

"Why, Evan's sister."

The name sent sparks running through Vivian's fingers. Jake's words came back to her: *Don't walk into other people's dark rooms.* But she felt certain this dark room belonged to her in some way. "Tell me about Evan." Her heart fluttered. From the corner of her eye, she saw Jake's hands curl into fists in his lap.

Ruth rose. "I shall go for a walk. I have no wish to be present when your box bursts open."

"Yes, dear, a walk will do you good," Bertha lamented.

When Ruth had gone, Vivian took her hand. "I seem to have disturbed your daughter."

"She doesn't want me to be hurt," the woman said. "But I'm happy. We had such jolly times, Grace and I, oh, I'm so happy!"

She grinned at her. "Yes, we had jolly times in the park, on the pier, at the fish market—"

"I can hardly imagine Grandmother at a fish market," Jake said softly.

"Every Sunday." Bertha leaned forward. "One day, Grace and Loretta agreed to help some woman with her stall."

"Grandmother sold fish in the fish market?" Vivian asked.

Bertha studied her. "She would have agreed to any adventure then."

"Is that why Grace came here?" Vivian looked at the blurry water. "For adventure?"

"Indeed, yes," Bertha was suddenly acute. "Young women often went to Europe and other places as a last fling before they settled into the business of marriage. It was no sin, no sin at all."

Jake rose and, with his hands shoved in his pockets, strolled down the pier in the opposite direction of where Ruth had gone.

Vivian felt her heart pulse with sadness. "He doesn't want to be hurt either."

"Some souls are more sensitive than others." Bertha sighed. "I can see why he was Grace's favorite. Yes, I can see that."

"Grace didn't go to Europe, did she?" Vivian persevered. "She came here instead."

"She needed a rest, child," Bertha said. "She stayed with us at first and then later— "

"She went to seek her own adventures," Vivian finished. The last word burned in her veins. She suddenly liked the idea of the woman in the parlor portrait hiding an adventuress behind her calm smile.

Bertha looked angry for the first time. "There was nothing tawdry about it!"

"I never meant to imply there was." Vivian squeezed her hand.

"Grace may have had strange notions, but she was sweet and generous!" The woman clutched her arm. "Oh, child, what am I saying? It's been so long since I've spoken of the past." She was quiet for a few moments. "She thought fish were sacred, truly she did. She even said they were magical. Yes, magical!"

"This man Evan, did he teach her how to draw fish?"

"Heavens, no, he hated the sight of the creatures!" She laughed. "He called them frozen subjects. And he was hardly a *man*. We took him for a boy of seventeen. but I suspect he was older."

"How old was Grace?"

"Nineteen." Red spots appeared on her cheeks. "She went with them, yes, indeed. Oh, she was always refined, always poised, even later, when —" She stared at the bay with troubled eyes. "She stayed with them for a time, but she came back to us as we always knew she would."

"Who was 'them'?"

"The artists at the colony."

"Brandywine." Vivian's hands pressed against the boards.

"Oh, you've heard of it?"

"You mentioned it yesterday."

"Did I?" The woman blinked.

"Someone else told me about it," Vivian said.

"Yes, well, she went for a visit, you see, and a week or so later, she went back there to stay." Tears filled the elderly woman's eyes.

Vivian studied her. "You didn't like him, did you? Evan, I mean."

"Oh, it wasn't that, child," she insisted. "It was only we thought he was — well, a bit of a derelict."

"Every young man has foolish ways," Vivian murmured. "Every young woman, for that matter."

"No, not that, not foolish." Bertha held up the glass lying on the pier. "Nebulous. That's what Malcolm called him. He used words like that in those days. Words you had to sneak into your father's study and look up." She chuckled.

"My grandfather said that?" She stared at her.

"Yes, he was quite a talker then." She shook her head. "He didn't seem to want to talk much yesterday. Poor man."

"In what way was Evan nebulous?" Vivian asked.

"He read Browning and Byron, that sort of thing." Her eyes danced. "Can you imagine? Poetry at a fish market?"

Vivian tried to envision this young man enticing her grandmother with poetry in a crowded fish market. How different he must have been from stoic, disciplined Grandfather! Why, then, had Grandmother chosen Grandfather over Even?

Ruth returned with her features aligned and calm. "I see your brother has more sense than you do."

"He's still a boy," Vivian said, glancing at Jake, now out of earshot at the end of the pier, staring out at the water.

"We were just talking about Evan, dear." Bertha turned to Vivian. "He gave Grace books on Browning and Byron while she was at Brandywine. She left them behind, I think. Oh, so many things she left behind. As if she didn't want to remember." The woman sighed as the water washing against the rocks. "She brought them with her when she came back to us. She used to read them to me." Her eyes became muddy. "'When glided in Porphyria; straight/She shut the cold out and the storm,/And kneeled and made the cheerless grate/Blaze up, and all the cottage warm.'"

"You have a remarkable memory, Mama," Ruth said.

Vivian sat back. "Were they — lovers?" She let the last fall boldly.

"Heavens, no!" Bertha became angry again. "Grace was not that kind of young lady."

"It was forty or fifty years ago." Ruth pointed out. "It could hardly matter now whether they were or weren't."

"You don't understand." Vivian laid her hand on the boards, feeling the warmth of the sun through the thick black glove. "I'm nineteen and going out into the world, dramatic as that may sound."

Ruth mumbled. "I think I'm beginning to."

"I can't go out into the world until I know who I really am," continued Vivian. "My brother can't take his place in the world either until he knows who he is. To know that, we must know who *she* was."

"Yes, yes," Bertha murmured. "How may one know where one is to go if one doesn't know where one has been?" She gave her daughter a sharp look. "I've told you that, Ruthie."

Her daughter said nothing, observing a seagull perched on a stump.

"We all thought he was infatuated with her," Bertha admitted. "But it was the sort of infatuation one would expect when a roguish but charming young man meets a refined young lady."

"Did you believe she infatuated with him as well?"

"In the beginning, perhaps. But later, I don't know. She was there an awful long time, and then she wasn't, and he wanted her to come back but she wouldn't."

Vivian felt her head spinning. "Was that because she was ill?"

"She wouldn't come back down to my party." The woman was off in her own world. "First there was the heat, oh, that unendurable heat. But we all felt the heat, and none of us were ill. Except for Loretta, but she was always ill."

Ruth gave Vivian a sharp look as she gathered the dirty dishes in the basket.

"How long was my grandmother in Waxwood?" Vivian asked.

"Oh, quite a while," said Bertha vaguely.

"My mother told me she was here for the summer."

"Oh, no! It was Malcolm who came here for the summer."

Vivian felt her stomach tighten. "He came here because she was here?"

The woman chuckled. "He said he came for the fishing and the rest. But I never saw him with a fishing rod!"

"And Grace?"

"Oh, she was here at least a year."

"A year!"

"Oh, dear, well, if she hadn't gone to Brandywine for so long — my, but she stayed a long time there!"

"How long?" The wind almost blew her veil forward but she grabbed it in time.

"I don't know, child," Bertha said with a sigh. "It's the way of old people. The things we remember and the things we don't, oh, my."

"If she stayed so long," Vivian said thoughtfully, "she must have been happy."

"Why, I don't know." Bertha's entire face was gaunt. "She was ill, as I said, then she wasn't. She was ready to accept one proposal, then another — and then — she left!" Tears filled her eyes.

Vivian held her skirt down from a gust of wind. "You mean my grandfather proposed to her in Waxwood?"

"Miss Alderdice," Ruth said firmly. "My mother is tired."

"You said one proposal and then another," Vivian persisted.

"I don't know. I don't know!" Bertha gasped.

"I'm sorry," she said in a soft voice. "I don't mean to upset you."

"There is nothing more she can tell you," Ruth hissed. "Come, Mama, it's time for your rest."

Jake returned just in time to insist on taking the handles of the moveable chair in his hands. Just as he had gently wheeled her onto the steady sidewalk, Bertha blurted out as if awakening from a dream. "Why don't you go there?"

"Go where?" Vivian asked.

"Brandywine." Her voice was breathless. "She'll know."

"She?"

"Verina." The name fell like a scented rose from the older woman's lips.

"Evan's niece," Ruth said in a quiet voice.

A choking sound rose in the air, and Vivian realized it came from her brother.

"Everything is there. Everything." Bertha's face looked relaxed, as if she had found a solution to a great problem.

"Mama, Verina was only a child."

"Children see and hear. They see and hear everything! Go, go!"

Vivian stared back at the water where the light moved in a thin line. The wind cut against her dress, billowing like the arms of a ghost, the specter fighting to emerge.

"She won't be able to find it, Mama," Ruth insisted. "It's hidden in the wax woods."

Vivian turned to her. "Will you take us then?"

"No!" Jake's voice was a whispering gasp.

"My mother is tired," Ruth said in a ragged voice. "You've exhausted and troubled her with your memories of the past. I must get her home." She took the handles of the chair from Jake. "Please leave us alone."

"I can't." Vivian's throat was tight.

"Doors are closed. Doors are open," Bertha lamented in a shaking voice. "Oh, better to open the door!"

Ruth's eyes met her mother's and held a steadfast gaze. Vivian's hands were damp under the heavy black gloves.

In a quiet voice, Ruth asked, "Mama, will it really give you peace of mind if I do this?"

"It will give her peace of mind," was the determined answer.

Her daughter's hands tightened. "Very well. But I'm taking you home first."

"We'll go with you," Vivian pulled her gloves on.

"I prefer to go alone, if you don't mind." The woman's tone was almost vicious. "You and your brother can wait for me here."

Vivian took Bertha's hand, limp and warm in hers. "Thank you. For everything."

The woman gave her a tender but hazy smile.

When the two women were out of sight up the street, Jake

grabbed her arm. A thundering expression made him look twice his age. "Viv, we can't do this!"

"We must do it," Vivian insisted. "You heard what Bertha said. Better to open the door."

"It's someone else's dark room." His voice broke. "It's *her* dark room."

"Whose?" Vivian looked at him. "Bertha's? Or Grace's?"

"Our grandmother's name was Penelope." His face turned pale.

She wretched free from him. "I see. So you're going to follow Mother's lead after all. File this away under the Unmentionables."

"I'm going home," he declared. "Won't you come with me?"

Vivian suddenly felt as tired as Ruth had looked. "Yes, I suppose it's best for you to go home. You've plenty of time to catch the train back to the city."

"I want you to come with me." This time, his tone was assertive.

She looked at him, amused. "You're already beginning to sound like Grandfather."

"Will you?"

She held both his hands. "I can't, darling. And you know why."

His head bowed down, staring at the uneven wooden panels on the pier. "What do I tell Mother?"

"Don't tell her anything," Vivian said firmly. "I'll tell her when I get back."

"She'll — she'll be angry."

Vivian couldn't help but grimace. "Perhaps I'll cast our specter into the waters before I get back. She'll be glad of that, won't she?"

She watched him dragging his feet down the dusty street, the sun casting a tall, slender shadow behind him.

CHAPTER 7

*R*uth returned, having put on a new hat and a shawl over her shoulders. "Where's Mr. Alderdice?"

"He had to go back to the city," Vivian mumbled.

"I see." There was an almost evil smile on her face. "Perhaps you ought to have gone with him."

Vivian gave her a defiant look. "I'm not afraid to walk into other people's dark rooms, Ruth."

"No," she said shortly, "I don't suppose you are."

She and Ruth walked in silence all the way back to the pier and took a skeletal ferry to the other side where the hills loomed majestically over the small town. "The colony is well hidden, isn't it?" she remarked as they stepped off the ferry.

Ruth shrugged. "Their way of life differs from ours in the 'civilized' world. They've become afraid of people."

She led Vivian down a narrow but well-marked path. The beauty of the hills presented a contrast of deep green with purple, and red wildflowers.

Feeling the greenery press in around her, Vivian said in a nervous tone, "Some cultures celebrate the dead, don't they?"

Ruth breathed heavily. "So I've heard."

"Perhaps they're right," Vivian said.

"You mean extol the life rather than bewail the death?" Ruth considered this. "I suppose it depends on the life. Your reverend had much to praise your grandmother, Miss Alderdice."

"Won't you call me Vivian?" she asked. "After today, we're no longer enemies."

"We were never enemies."

"Then we ought to be friends," Vivian said firmly.

Ruth considered this as well as the silence of the grassy hill shut out the singing of birds. "We're not friends either. But I will call you Vivian if you wish."

The tightness in Vivian's chest eased. "Tell me about Brandywine."

"According to Mama, it was a thriving community when your grandmother was there," said Ruth. She produced a coarse handkerchief and wiped her forehead. "Was Grace so unhappy with the San Francisco swells?"

Vivian's instinct was to tell the truth, but it seemed disloyal to her grandmother. And yet, she couldn't bring herself to utter another lie. "She had her place."

"Oh, Mama told me of that life," said Ruth. "Waxwood had its swells too back then." She was quiet for a moment. "And your mother? Has she her place among them as well?"

"Of course."

"And now you shall take your place," Ruth lamented.

Vivian hadn't thought of it as her "place", but she could not deny it. She would, like her grandmother and mother, soon be another angel in the house and in San Francisco society.

"I don't recall seeing your father at the funeral," Ruth continued.

The bumpy path dug into Vivian's shoes. "My mother is a widow."

"Oh, I'm sorry," Ruth said.

"It was a long time ago," she said. "I was a baby when my father died, and Jake was only three when his went away."

"Went away?"

"Died, I mean, died," she said quickly.

They both trudged up the hill for a few moments in silence. Then, Ruth said, "The obituary called Grace a 'celebrated socialite and a benevolent lady.' Was she?"

Vivian raised an eyebrow. "You seem very interested in my grandmother all of a sudden."

"It was you who opened the Pandora's box," Ruth snapped. "Remember that."

"Yes," Vivian said in a steely voice. "She was all those things the obituary said."

"I can't imagine Malcolm Alderdice was a simple man to please," Ruth chuckled. "Perhaps social success was the only way to do so."

Vivian's forehead dampen, and she reached for the handkerchief in her sleeve. "Yes, perhaps that's why Grandmother let her art fall by the wayside when she married Grandfather."

"My mother told me society ladies often trifled with paints or piano keys or even pen and paper," the woman observed.

"Yes, my mother told me that too," Vivian murmured.

"But she said that was all they did. Dilly-dallied about for their amusement."

Vivian's crumpled the lace handkerchief. "But my grandmother might not have wanted to dilly-dally about, is that it?"

"Mama said she stayed at Brandywine for a long time," Ruth pointed out. "I believe one can surmise she took it seriously enough to want to learn from those more experienced than she."

"But my grandfather had no wish to stop her," said Vivian. "Your mother said as much."

"Not before their marriage perhaps," said the woman. "But after—" She stepped over a pile of rocks in the path.

Vivian stiffened. "You judge my grandfather when you know nothing about him."

"I know enough about him from what my mother told me," said Ruth, "Back in the days when she wasn't so confused."

"He loved Grandmother," Vivian said stubbornly. "He built a house on a hill just for her."

"One's castle may also be one's cage."

Vivian glared at her. "Alderdice Hall *was* my grandmother's castle, not her cage." The words sounded hollow and hesitant. "Naturally, her duties changed when she married Grandfather."

"More's the pity," Ruth mumbled.

Vivian stumbled against a rock, thrusting her arms out to break her fall. She sat on the ground, looking at Ruth. "Most people don't understand my grandfather. He came from nothing and worked his way up in business and society. If you could see him now—" She bit her lip as she remembered Ruth had seen him in his dazed state at the funeral.

The woman held out her arm, and helped her up. She said in a soft voice, "We're in the wax wood forest."

The hill was now crowded with tall trees. Vivian slipped off a glove and touched the strange, glossy bark, the matted sheen sticky and rough.

"The surface softens with the sun and hardens with the moon," Ruth said. "It's why they call them wax wood trees."

They ascended into a dense mesh of those strange trees into a carpet of green clover and purple berries.

"Lovely, isn't it?" Ruth sounded hushed and sweet.

"They chose a wonderful place for their colony," Vivian remarked.

"They didn't choose it for its beauty." The woman scowled. "No one comes to see the wax wood forest anymore."

"Perhaps there were more visitors forty years ago," she suggested.

The woman smirked. "Even the easy-going Californians would have thought them too wild and hedonic for their taste."

Vivian tried not to think of the woman from the parlor portrait, in her naive pink and tulle, among the wax wood trees with those wild and hedonistic artists. She adjusted the veil protectively over her face.

They reached the gate where a small hut stood displaying paintings and sculptures outside with paper tags. Vivian ducked as she entered so that her hat would not brush against the low ceiling. The cave-like room could not hide the festival of art. Sliding glass doors opened out to a small garden with larger sculptures.

"Built not long after your grandmother left," Ruth informed her.

A woman with a cherubic face was in the garden. She wore a brown dress finished with coral beads around the hem and sleeves. Rather than swept back in the latest style, her dark hair gathered into a thick braid that swung over her shoulder as she leaned forward. Her informality made Vivian feel stifled in her weeds, and she lifted her veil to feel the cool air on her skin.

Ruth motioned for her to remain while she proceeded to the garden. Vivian could not hear the words, but the warm tone penetrated through the glass door. Vivian guessed the woman was Evan's niece. The woman listened with great intensity, a watering can poised in her hand. She looked at Vivian in a way that made Vivian's skin feel clammy. For a moment, she regretted having agreed to the excursion. What right had she to come to this strange, isolated place, overdressed, overly formal, and surely unwanted?

Then she remembered her purpose. The Alderdice in her asserted its privilege as she strolled out to the garden and said in a loud but friendly voice, "Good afternoon. I hope I'm not intruding."

She put the pail down. "I welcome visitors. Miss Alderdice, is it?" She held out her hand.

"Please call me Vivian," she said. "And I may call you Verina?"

"Why not?" Her voice was as childlike as her face.

"I imagine it gets rather lonely here for you," Vivian remarked.

"Oh, there are plenty of people about." Verina wrapped a thick shawl around her shoulders. "Only they usually prefer their own kind."

"You'r not an artist yourself?" Vivian asked.

The woman's face reddened against the natural light. "No."

"Vivian can be very frank at times," Ruth said with that touch of viciousness.

The woman asked. "You are interested in artists?"

"I'm interested in my grandmother."

"Was she an artist here?"

Vivian glanced at Ruth. "My grandmother is — was — Penelope Alderdice."

"I don't know the name." She pulled her shawl closer to her as a fresh breeze slipped into the garden.

"I believe you knew her as Grace Carlyle."

Verina swayed a little, and her face turned pale Vivian produced a small bottle of smelling salts from her reticule. "I'm all right," the woman insisted. "Ruth told me you're from San Francisco, and you were interested in Uncle Evan."

"I'm sorry, dear," said Ruth. "I ought to have mentioned Vivian is Grace's granddaughter."

Vivian felt her anger rise. "I see Ruth didn't explain the real reason for my coming here."

Verina, clearly recovered, stiffened. "I can tell you nothing about your grandmother."

"Nothing?" Vivian stared at the smooth face.

"I recall little of my childhood." The woman would not look at her. "I barely remember the name."

"You can tell her about Evan," Ruth said in a soft voice.

"She didn't even know Uncle Evan!"

Vivian took her hands. "I'd like to know about him. Please."

The woman's eyes clawed at her face. "I understand this Penelope Alderdice just passed away."

"How did you know that?"

The woman did not answer. She only repeated, "I have nothing to tell you."

"Vivian wants to know about Grace and her time here." Ruth's voice was even softer than before.

Verina snarled. "I leave the past in the past."

"I can't do that." Vivian's eyes filled with tears.

"Mama asked me to bring her to you," Ruth put her arm around the woman's shoulders. "She thought you might know more than we do."

"I know nothing!"

"That's not true!"

Vivian appealed to Verina, her hands pressed together. "If you truly know nothing, I shall leave right now and never disturb you again. But if you know anything at all about my grandmother, I beg you to tell me. It concerns more lives than mine." She thought of her brother.

The woman wavered. "We can't speak here." She glanced at the door. "If someone should come in — they don't like to remember my uncle."

"Perhaps you might take Vivian home and offer her tea?" Ruth suggested.

Verina smiled for the first time. "My house is small, Vivian, but hospitable."

Ruth sighed. "I must get back. I've left Mama alone for too long as it is."

"No, come for tea too!" A look of terror appeared in her friend's eyes.

"Don't be afraid of Vivian, dear." Ruth said gently. "She's not a bit haughty or conceited."

"Thank you." Vivian bowed of her head.

"I suppose we shall see you again?" Ruth glanced at her.

The veiled invitation touched Vivian. "I'd like that. I hope to see the mermaid."

"Mermaid?" Verina glanced at her friend.

"The drawing Grace made for Mama's twentieth birthday," Ruth said.

"Yes." Her voice was soft. "Yes, the birthday party." The round features on Verina's face turned sharp and ethereal, and Vivian imagined this was what the vixen that the architect saw in the dust of Alderdice Hall had looked like.

CHAPTER 8

*V*erina led her down the colony's main path. Spare shacks stood on either side, and a grim faces peered out the window of one of them as they passed. The open stare made Vivian pull her veil back over her face. "They don't like you much, do they?"

"Uncle Evan and I lived in San Francisco for five years before we came back here," said Verina. "They don't take kindly to dissenters." She looked ahead. "It wasn't like that when I was a child. We couldn't sit in the garden without half the colony visiting us."

"I see why you speak of *they* and not *us*," Vivian said.

Verina glanced at her. "Ruthie said you were inquisitive. I see you're insightful too."

"Insightful people are intelligent," Vivian said grimly. "I've had no decent education beyond what my brother calls the 'feminine fineries.' I try to read as much as I can, though."

"You are frank," Verina said with a smile. "I hadn't much education either. It was Grace who encouraged me to read."

Vivian thought the library at Alderdice Hall and the times she had seen Grandmother looking at them with longing, then turn away as if they reminded her of something unpleasant.

"She read voraciously when she lived with us," Verina continued. "She wanted me to read with her, but I couldn't read very well, so I asked her to tell me the story. She was a beautiful storyteller." Her eyes became bright with memory. "Mama was furious at her for it."

"Why?" Vivian asked.

"I don't remember."

"I ought to have brought some books with me," Vivian said. "We have so many and no one really reads them anymore."

Verina stared down the path. "They wouldn't have accepted them here, and neither would I."

"How do they make a living?"

"Commissions, mostly," said Verina. "They do a little sketching when the tourists come for the summer. Caricatures and that sort of thing."

"And you," Vivian asked, "how do you live?"

She smiled ruefully. "I earn a little from my work at the store."

"Is there no one to help you?"

"The Waxwood Ladies Society brings food and blankets now and then, but the artists won't touch them."

"So you don't either." Vivian tried to avoid looking at the woman's ragged dress and shawl. "You mustn't starve because of their pride. You've a right to take care of yourself." Verina's lips tightened "Forgive me for interfering, but you seemed so unhappy here."

The woman drew her shawl closer around her narrow shoulders. "Uncle Evan was happy here. He would have wanted me to stay."

"And so you stay?"

Verina's hand tightened under Vivian's arm. "One does not leave the life one has known for so long easily or willingly."

Vivian thought of how she and Jake used to steal into the library to look at the atlas and whisper of all the places they would visit one day. Vivian loved the solitude of the Swiss Alps, while Jake wanted the exoticism of the Nile. And, yet, it seemed inconceivable to her to leave Alderdice Hall. "I could help you," she suddenly said.

Verina was silent.

"I know a woman who's done some work with shop girls."

"Charity work." The woman glared at her.

"Yes," Vivian admitted. "I'm sure she could get you a position in San Francisco."

"I've no wish to leave here."

"But you're an outsider." In a softer voice, she heard herself say, "I know what it feels like to be an outsider."

"I must stay." The tone was final. "I *must* stay."

They reached a small fork in the road with a house that looked a little sturdier and larger than the rest. "Uncle Evan used to live like the others," said Verina. "When Mama and I came to live with him, he tore it down and built this one." Her face was soft with memories. "They had a hard life. Mama was like a mother to him."

The cottage looked as if it were built with exactitude and affection. The boards were expertly constructed to keep out wind and rain, and the roof was of Swiss-style red tile that peaked at the center. Vivian could not keep the admiration out of her eyes as she stared at it.

"He told us he traveled through towns along the peninsula and made caricatures for pennies to save enough for the roof," Verina said with pride.

The space inside was no bigger than the Alderdice Hall chapel. Vivian could not help thinking how it hardly suited two adults, much less three and a child. As if reading her mind, Verina said. "Grace slept in Mama's room with me."

"And your mother?"

"Mama preferred sleeping on the covered porch with her

sculptures. She didn't mind. She thought of them almost as her friends."

Vivian pulled off her gloves as she took a few steps into the living room, dining room, and parlor all in one.

"Shall I open a window? It can get rather stuffy in here."

The room's nakedness made it feel more vast than it was, and with the late afternoon breeze lifted the burden of her mourning. Had Grace loved being in this room? It felt like a small airy box. But then, Grandmother had *wanted* Alderdice Hall with its massive rooms and high ceilings where one's voice always echoed. She had insisted on cramming every room with cushions and *objets d'art*. According to Grandfather, she had wanted all those things. What could have changed her?

Verina emerged from the kitchen carrying a tray in her hands. "I can tell you very little about Grace. But I'll try to answer your questions." Her manner sounded too composed to Vivian's ears.

"How old were you when my grandmother came to Waxwood?" Vivian asked.

"I was, oh, four years old. Possibly younger."

Vivian eyed her. "And yet you already knew how to read."

"I might have been five or six."

"When did she come to the colony?"

"Not long after Christmas. I don't remember the exact year."

Vivian looked down at the rug. It had a peculiar pattern of faceless penguins "If you were six years old—"

"1852," she answered quietly. "Uncle Evan invited her to visit. It was to be only a visit."

"But she ended up staying," said Vivian. "I remember Mrs. Ross telling me that." She folded her hands in her lap. "How long did she stay?"

"Oh, months," said Verina.

"Months, or months and months?"

The woman hesitated. "I don't remember. She left in the summer. I remember that."

Vivian examined the pillow. "She came after Christmas of '52, so she must have stayed until the summer of '53. That would make it six months at least." She looked down at Verina. "Mrs. Ross said she came back to town and stayed with her."

"Yes," said Verina. "It was a long, boiling summer."

Vivian grasped a tassel. "Now why did she do that? Go back to town, I mean?"

"I don't know." Verina began rocking. "I imagine Grace's high-toned friends were missing her."

"Do you really believe that?" She peered at the woman.

"Is there any reason I shouldn't?" The voice rose.

"How was she when she left?" Vivian asked. "In your child's eye. Happy? Angry? Melancholy?"

"She was always cheerful," Verina said. "She loved everything and everyone." She began rearranging the tea things.

"Then," Vivian said in a careful voice, "she would have had no reason to leave, would she?"

The sugar bowl knocked against the teapot. "Unless she had more attractive prospects in town."

"Her friends, you mean?"

"Other prospects."

Vivian frowned. "Marriage prospects."

Verina sat back. "Grace could be a bit of a flirt."

Vivian ignored this. "I understand my grandfather was in Waxwood that summer too."

The woman's hands drew away from the tray. "Yes."

"Did my grandfather ever meet your uncle while he was here?" Vivian asked. "Perhaps in town?"

"Oh, yes," said the woman.

"Did you ever meet him?"

Verina shrugged. "We were all at the Fourth of July picnic. I'm sure I met him then, but I don't recall."

Vivian watched Verina wrap her arms around her knees, her eyes arched and distant.

"You remember something," Vivian said.

"I think Uncle Evan and your grandfather knew one another from before."

"In San Francisco."

"No, elsewhere."

"Why do you say that?" Vivian tried to catch the woman's eye.

"Once a man came to speak to Uncle Evan. He was well-dressed and very imposing."

Vivian felt a jolt. "Was this before or after Grace went back to town?"

"You're questioning me as if I've committed some kind of crime." She grabbed the tray and disappeared.

Vivian followed her into a warm, tiny kitchen that smelled of fresh mint. "Forgive me if I'm being insensitive. All this has been a painful shock to me. First my grandmother's death, and then discovering she was someone else, someone very different from the woman I believed her to be."

Verina grasped her hand, her touch strong with resentment.

"Mrs. Ross told me my grandmother was ill that summer."

"I know nothing of that." The tone was sharp. "I've told you all I know. Now, if you'll excuse me, I've work to do." She turned to the dishes.

"I'm sorry if I've upset you," said Vivian. "I won't trouble you further with questions. If you'll permit me to ask to see a picture of your uncle, I'll be on my way."

Verina blinked. "Why do you want it?"

"He was part of my grandmother's life once," she remained her. "It's natural I should want to see what a friend of hers looked like, isn't it?"

Verina seemed reluctant to move her hands out from the basin. "I might have a self portrait or a drawing one of the artists made of him."

Vivian squeezed her shoulder kindly. "I realize this is difficult."

The woman dried her hands. "I suppose it's more difficult for you than for me."

Verina brought out a large box. Despite its size, it contained precious little. Vivian examined two drawings and one painting hardly larger than a book. They had faded with time, so they showed only an outline of a man. "It isn't much of a legacy," she lamented.

"One hardly needs pictures to remember a beloved uncle," Verina said stiffly.

Vivian nodded. "I'm sure he must have been very handsome."

Verina sat on the floor in front of the box as if guarding it. "He had a rather ordinary face. But he drew people around him. Mama used to say he was the devil's charmer."

"I can see how he would have enchanted my grandmother."

"Many ladies liked him, Mama said."

"Yet he fell in love with *her*."

"That's nonsense. Nonsense!"

Vivian crushed the cushion of the comfortable chair as the coo of a dove slipped into the room from some far off tree, leaving a haunting echo. "I shall go." As she rose, her foot tipped the box to one side, spilling pages on the rug. Verina grab them, but Vivian's hand reached first. They weren't papers but letters, a small packet that had been tied loosely with a piece of twine. The handwriting was familiar.

"She wrote letters!"

"Please." Verina's hands came together.

Vivian could not take her eyes off the envelopes. They were addressed to Joanna Carlyle in San Francisco.

"So my grandmother wrote her mother while she was in Waxwood," Vivian murmured. "Where did you get them?"

"Turn them, over." Verina's lips were strained.

Vivian saw a note attached in the front: *I asked my mother to give these to you. They are the last. Your Grace.*

Tears filled her eyes for the woman who had sought this sanctuary in the woods. She held out the packet, but Verina drew back. "I don't want them now! I never wanted them."

"They belonged to your Uncle Evan."

"He never wanted them either." Verina's voice was almost a whisper. "He never looked at them." She sat erect now. "Take them with you, or I'll burn them as I should have done years ago."

"I can't read them at home." Vivian's hands trembled. "Is there a place I can go where I can think?"

Almost reluctantly, Verina said, "You may stay here if you wish."

Vivian held the woman's hands in hers. "You would do that after the pain I've caused you?"

"I can do nothing else," she said in a defeated voice.

When silence filled the small room Verina gave her and only the hoot of owls in far-off trees let out vague screeches outside her window, Vivian unwrapped the twine from the letters.

CHAPTER 9

Waxwood, CA August 30, 1852

*D*earest Mama,
    I arrived safely in Waxwood yesterday evening. I am a little weak and have been resting most of the day. There have already been a fair number of visitors so I feel almost as if I never left home! I've met most of the young people worth meeting in Waxwood. Bertha has been bouncing in and out of the parlor all day, pulling some young lady or gentleman after her. She says they are all curious about San Francisco. They ask me a lot of questions, but I suspect they only half-believe me when I tell them San Francisco is as virtuous as Waxwood. They are all so kind and thoughtful that I've had none of my melancholic musings.

    I am grateful you and Papa allowed me to come to Waxwood alone. I know how surprised you were when I said I wanted to come here. What young lady of Rincon Hill would forgo the joys of Paris, Venice, and London for a secluded seaside town nearer to home? But I have wanted to see Waxwood for so long. Papa's stories of his youth among the wax wood trees enchanted me so. Little did I fathom this quaint little community has its own exclusive circle no less elegant than ours on Rincon Hill! Despite its congenial people, I feel certain there is an adventure waiting for me.

I know I shall get my strength back soon. You may tell Dr. Cumberland I no longer have chills, fatigue, or nightmares. They have disappeared now that I'm here. I don't dislike Rincon Hill, and I am aware I have obligations to you and to our society. But I know you'll understand when I tell you I felt crushed under the weight of those obligations. For one may find even the most pleasant society a stone on one's heart when one is beset with prying eyes looking for every stumble, every misplaced word and uncouth social grace. No one is more vulnerable to their scrutiny than a debutante.

I wish I could have explained it so well when I insisted on going away on my own. It's one thing for Papa to speak of wanting to make something of himself in a city of opportunities like San Francisco. That's all well and good and as it should be for a man. But we women are chained to our ornaments and fineries. My life as of late has been one long round of luncheons, balls, soirees, and fittings, pushing toward the next marital opportunity. It's all the young ladies of Rincon Hill talk about, and most seem to delight in the game. But my head aches so from the surveillance.

How different it was when I was a child! There were always new amusements, and no hand held me back. I was as free as Tommy Blight and Ellis Merrimand and the other boys. I could draw pictures as much as I liked, and no one looked down their noses at me for being a "bohemian." But since my coming out, I have lost that. I have watched one by one as the young girls I grew up with turned into young ladies, languishing on garden swings and conservatory settees, lips silent, eyes picking up cues from their mothers and aunts on how to be gracious and docile and how to flirt modestly. I vowed it would not be so when my turn came. But I have been just as languid as they.

I feel sure that's what caused this strange illness, Mama. Not my "nerves," as Dr. Cumberland claims. For what are nerves, really, but a more vibrant version of yourself screaming out?

I tell you all this so you may see why I was headstrong about coming here alone. I feel certain if I had stayed in the city, I would have married the first boorish youth who asked me and made everyone, including myself, most unhappy. I would have been even more dead in my soul than I am now.

You cannot imagine how blue the sky is in Waxwood! There is none of the grayness of the city fog. That formidable enemy does not blanket the windows in the morning, and the mist does not seep through in the evening, making flowers look like steel figures. At night, you can see the stars, oh, what stars! I remember Papa pointing them out to me when I was but too young to remember their names. Now Bertha and I sit on the porch swing and look at them. Neither she nor I have any idea which is which. Dear Bertha with her little knotted mind, but always so kind and generous!

It is strange how an open sky can make one feel so limitless. Earlier this evening, I sat alone on the veranda looking at the tiny houses and thinking how different it all is! San Francisco is like a crystal castle in comparison, majestic with its hills and ships in the harbor. The homes on Rincon Hill cut into the sky with their lofty towers. One never realizes how compressed it all is until one walks down Market Street into the heart of the city.

Waxwood is almost like an island at the end of a peninsula. The modest pier has two sides, and one never knows where one will end up. When I arrived, I left my baggage at the Rosses and walked the entire wooden walkway. I didn't know where the turn would lead me once I followed its whims, and then I realized I was at the other end of Main Street! Once I get my strength back, I will draw it for you.

Everyone here is so amiable. They say they remember Papa, although I am sure some do not. Mrs. Bowling keeps squinting at me as if I look familiar, but Loretta says squinting is her general affectation and I should take no notice. The young ladies are all so sweet — Selma, Laura, Mary, Patricia, Loretta and, of course, Bertha. Selma insists we call ourselves "the Belles of Waxwood" and give parties, and arrange picnics and boat trips with all the young gentlemen in the county. She predicts we shall all be engaged by the time we are twenty.

How ironic! It is precisely what I have come here to avoid, at least for the time being. I seek peace even in company. I feel sure I shall not get lost.

Your loving daughter, Penelope

CHAPTER 10

Waxwood, CA September 9, 1852

*D*earest Mama,

It's strange to think one year ago today, we ceased to think of ourselves as Californians and began seeing ourselves as Americans. Perhaps you find it strange to hear me talk about such things. No doubt if Papa were to read this letter, he would think it preposterous. Has he not worked hard so you and I need only concern ourselves with the latest Paris and New York frocks and other feminine frivolities and not complicated matters such as statehood?

I have opened my eyes to so many things since I've been in Waxwood. It's not only the men who speak of politics and business and the ways of the world here but the women too. It is so unlike Rincon Hill where it is considered in poor taste for a young lady to discuss politics, much less know anything about the world in which she lives.

No doubt it is business as usual in the city now. I imagine the ladies scurrying down Market Street, their veils close to their faces to avoid the dust, and their maids trailing after them, clutching parcels so as not to let them fall and risk a scolding. Men sit in cable cars with the *Alta California* spread on their laps. Mothers herd their children home, leaving a spinning top or a doll on the front steps.

In Waxwood, no one rushes about putting on airs. As this is a holiday, no one has taken a step inside a shop or school all day. Children were running around the park when we all set out after lunch, though not in the frightening way children do in the city, running out into the roads just when the horses approach and ducking under cabs in jest or dare. Perhaps the coastal air makes them less impish. They are obedient children on the whole, not with their noses in the air like the younger siblings of the girls we know. Loretta's sister, Flossie, picked all the wildflowers she could find and made lovely chains with them for all the Belles.

Besides the children, the men out in the streets, old, young, decrepit, all with smiles on their faces as if what awaited them back at the office or in the shop needn't concern them for the moment. The women hung on their arms as if proud to have someone in attendance.

There were at least half a dozen groups like ours when we arrived at the park. Bertha and I brought angel food cake, someone else brought wine, another fruit, and so on. We gathered around the gazebo and had our little feast. I don't remember half the names of the people I met and I daresay Bertha, who introduced them to me, would be unable to match names to faces if I were to ask her though she has lived with them all her life. Dear, sweet Bertha. The little bird with her old-fashioned, kind-hearted ways.

Most of the Belles of Waxwood are fishermen's daughters, and what they will do to catch the eye of a young man! They are more brazen than Charlotte or Kate or Billie or Rachel back home. Their coquetry is of a different kind than the girls in San

Francisco. They do not hide behind their fans, giggle incessantly, or avoid sipping their punch too quickly. They join heartily in conversations, even serious ones. I remain silent as a lamb like Bertha because I feel ashamed of my ignorance.

Today at the picnic, a recently published book was the subject of debate in which the ladies took part as much as the men. They used words like "abolitionist" and "Fugitive Slave Act" and I felt foolish not knowing what they were talking about.

Selma turned to me and asked what they were saying about *Uncle Tom's Cabin* in the city. They all looked at me expectedly. I wished I were ice so that the sun might melt me right there and then, Mama. For what has abolitionism to do with the frocks and gossip we speak of behind our fans at the soirees and luncheons on Rincon Hill?

"I do not believe in slavery," I said to them.

"Naturally," Selma said. "But what of everyone else in San Francisco? What do the newspapers say?"

I felt at that moment as if I had a thousand eyes upon me. I stuttered so as I pointed out we ought to know our own minds without the influence of the press.

There were a few soft murmurs, but most were silent. Loretta came to my rescue by saying, "My papa always says, 'lead with your heart and others shall follow.'" The young gentlemen and ladies nodded and moved on to another topic. It was not until the sun had set that my embarrassment diminished and I could join the others with more ease and confidence.

I wish you could have seen the sun setting over the hills, as it was so beautiful. All autumn shades replace the brilliant blue. I almost wish I had brought my sketchbook.

Your loving daughter, Penelope

CHAPTER 11

Waxwood, CA September 20, 1852

*D*earest Mama,
    I love the serenity here at the Rosses. Mr. Ross doesn't retire to the study after dinner among his papers but sits with the rest of us in the parlor smoking his pipe (he always asks me if the smoke will disturb me before he lights it, which, of course, it does not — it reminds me of Papa and brings a little tender feeling in my heart). He reads the *Waxwood Review* as closely as Papa reads the *Alta California*. If a story provokes his anger, he growls and rails against the writer as if he were standing in front of the fireplace awaiting retribution. If the story is happy, he smiles with glee, and if it is amusing, he chuckles aloud as he reads.

    Mrs. Ross reads too. I don't believe I've ever seen a woman more engrossed with reading than she. Why, the bookcase in our study is nothing compared to that in her bedroom. Can you imagine, Mama? Where other women have closets with clothes and shoes, she has three bookcases that reach the ceiling!

Every evening, just as we're finishing dinner, we hear Hannah, Mrs. Ross' personal maid, on the stairs. She goes into the parlor and puts one of those thick books on the chair where Mrs. Ross always sits. She then arranges the pillows and the lace afghan, folding it neatly so Mrs. Ross may spread it across her lap if the night is chilly. Mr. Ross looks at his wife with one of his congenial smiles and says, "My dear, your peculiarity puts me aghast." She smiles at him and her raises as if to acknowledge his misnomer. Bertha shrugs and continues with her dessert. As for myself, sometimes I am amused, sometimes a little put out, perhaps from jealousy.

Ever since Admissions Day, I have been interested in Mrs. Ross' books. Tonight, as Bertha rattled on the piano, I asked Mrs Ross what she was reading. She looked quite startled, as no one in the house has ever shown an interest in her books before. She answered, "*Uncle Tom's Cabin.*"

"We were speaking of that book on Admissions Day." I turned to Bertha. "Remember?" The little canary had given up her tunes and moved to the couch, picking at the loops on the pattern I was crocheting, which I did not like. You know I don't fuss about things, but Bertha is so much the vacant bird she can unravel the tightest seams without half trying.

"Oh, it's wicked! Wicked, wicked Mrs. Stowe." And she shook a finger in the air, making her father laugh.

Her mother explained Mrs. Stowe is not a wicked woman, but writes of the wickedness of others.

"Is it not the same?" Bertha asked.

"No, indeed!" Mrs. Ross answered. "One may write or even speak of evil, such as Mrs. Stowe speaks of slavery, to expose it as such. That makes her good, not wicked."

I thought of the careless stories related at dinner parties about slavery on Rincon Hill, always cut short by the hostess so as not to offend the Southerners among us. Or else, we heard of it from the chatter of young men who are then scolded for speaking about such "unsavory" matters in front of ladies. I recalled my feelings of shame and ignorance at the picnic. I asked Mrs. Ross if I may read it.

Bertha, the dear old-fashioned thing, gasped and carried on, and even shook the crochet pattern at me as if to remind me my duty lay with pretty patterns and not books. Mr. Ross hesitated, mumbling about whether he ought to write to Papa and ask his permission. Even Mrs. Ross hinted that you and Papa would doubtless disapprove of such books.

"I am nineteen and can read what I wish," I reminded them all.

"Young ladies need not muddle their heads with anything as torrid as slavery," Mr. Ross murmured. "Oh, it's fine for *you* to read such things, Celeste. But young women like Penelope—"

"I don't see why young women like Penelope oughtn't to know what's going on in the world," Mrs. Ross interrupted. She patted my head and promised to lend it to me when she finished reading it.

So you see, Mama, your worries about to my health were for nothing. I am not languishing in melancholy, nor am I idle or bored. I am not only becoming quite the social butterfly, as much as one can be in a small town, but I am also shunning ignorance!

Your loving daughter, Penelope

CHAPTER 12

Waxwood, CA October 9, 1852

*D*earest Mama,
    I now know what the saying "ignorance is bliss" really means. There is something comforting about ignorance. Cloaked in ignorance, one may go about one's business seeing only the pleasantries in life, like the colors of the flowers and the wind walking on the water. Why, one may even ignore the twists and turns of life's tragedies if they have no direct affect. My own ignorance has been challenged, first with Mrs. Stowe's book, which I am now reading, and then with my encounter with the fisherwoman.

This morning, I awakened early and, feeling restless, I went for a walk a little after sunrise while the rest of the household slept. Oh, it was glorious to be out with no one about save the greengrocer collecting fresh produce off the wagon for the day. Even he did not seem to notice me, buried as he was in his work.

So it was just the sun and myself taking note of the beauty around us. Not a very healthy sun, to be sure. A rather pasty one, in fact. We were both braving the cool morning; she wrapped in firelight, and I wrapped in my cloak.

Lady Sun and I reached the pier, and what do you think, Mama? A woman was perched on the rocks, casting her line. We frightened one another half to death, I daresay, unexpected as the company of the other was. She looked gruff in her man's coat and trousers, her dirty blond hair waving in the wind and a smile that hid her eyes. She invited me to sit with her, promising me a "gay ole time." "Ladies like you ain't got but one thin layer o'skin," she said. "The wind takes 'way the warmth of *that*, sure 'nough."

"I am not like the other ladies," I said, recalling Mrs. Ross' words.

"P'rhaps not, but you're shiverin' like a cat in a gale." She took off her coat and handed it to me. Oh, she was very thoughtful, indeed. She even shared her breakfast of bread and cheese with me.

We had a long while to wait for the fish to bite, and in the meantime, she told me about herself. She did not ask if I wanted to hear her stories. She seemed hardly interested in who I was or where my business lay but assumed my business was to be her listening ear!

Her brusque manner put me off at first. She reminded me of some of those young men Papa introduced me to — Dan Weston, Nolan Saxon, and that young man who works for Papa, Malcolm Alderdice.

Despite her rough exterior, she goes by the dainty name of Kate Dalton. She was there to see the redfish. "Red and gold-eyed, as fine a gold as the coins in your father's purse, I reckon!" Then she grew sad and told me her father died three weeks ago. When I asked her why she was not in mourning, she said, "Ain't no use mournin' when one's got to live. He would turn in his grave 'fore he'd see me walking 'round in black, bawling into my 'kerchief."

Her speech was not wholly Californian, and she admitted she had been born in the East. Her father had been a black sheep in a family of preachers. Rather than take the cloth as his brothers had done, he went West, dragging her mother and Kate, a three-month-old child, with him. "We took the wagon train," she said. "'Course, bein' but a baby, I don't remember nothin'." In California, her father found work in a mercantile store in Sacramento, and within five years bought out the owner. "Yessir, he become a resp'ctful citizen." She almost spitting the words out.

"You speak as if being respectable were scandalous," I said.

This made her rock with laughter. "I've known some mighty evil people in my time who wore the badge of resp'ct as if they was the Lord."

Alas, her mother died, and left Kate to take care of the house. "I couldn't do book-learnin'"and run a house at the same time," she pointed out. "I use to read aloud to Pa every night 'cause his eyesight weren't so good." When her father died, she sold the store and now travels around, stopping to catch what fish she can for her breakfast and supper.

"It's the sadness of life, young 'un," she said to me. "You ain't got no one but you'self when you're born and when you die. Ain't no family gonna change that."

We caught two fish. I could see why she called them redfish. Their heads and fins were silver, but red velvet covered their bellies, and they gleamed with gold eyes and teeth, yes, teeth, Mama! Funny how it never occurred to me fish could have teeth.

I saw the redfish's wide-eyed glare in the eyes of Kate Dalton. Their wideness differs from Bertha's startled eyes. Hers come from naivety and ignorance while Kate's are always looking for the wonders of life. I shall be a Kate more than a Bertha if I can.

I'm including my drawing of the redfish, which hardly does justice to this little Tiresias.

. . .

Your loving daughter, Penelope

CHAPTER 13

Waxwood, CA October 31, 1852

*D*earest Mama,
   I have been in a melancholic mood all day, perhaps because it's Halloween. I went for a walk this morning, hoping to see Kate again, but the pier was deserted. Perhaps the fishermen feared the dusty fog hanging low over the roofs and treetops. I wanted to escape into the sunshine and almost took the stage-coach back to San Francisco, but my conscience would not allow me to abandon the Rosses and the others who have been so kind to me.

What was I trying to escape from? I thought at first it was the party planned for this evening. Since I have taken up reading, drawing and solitary walks along the pier, I have been shrugging off the Belles and their beaus, reveling in my solitude. The thought of a large, noisy party almost frightened me.

But I now believe it was something far simpler. The dungeon

atmosphere in Waxwood made my solitude unbearable, and I was more than thankful when it gave way to dusk. The jolly way in which the people here embrace Halloween lifted my spirits, and I was more than ready for company by evening.

Oh, how they play tricks here on All Hallows' Day!

I ought to have suspected something when Mrs. Ross insisted we finish our coffee on the veranda. No sooner had we settled ourselves when vagabonds and rickety old men and witches and goblins began parading down the street carrying small pumpkins carved with gruesome faces lit up inside by candles. They were children, of course, dressed in macabre costumes. One little boy hung his head over the fence and his mask was all distorted, as if someone had burned the poor boy's face. Poor boy indeed! He threw the pumpkin into the rosebush, and the candle fell out. The flame ate up a few of the blooms before the servants could remove it and put out the fire. I can still smell a little of the burned perfume through the open window.

Mr. Ross ran to the gate, shaking his fist at the boy. But when he returned he had a grin on his face. I joined in the laughter along with Mrs. Ross. My melancholy completely dissolved, and I felt happy again. But I cannot say the same of Bertha. The boy's prank disturbed the poor thing considerably. Dear old-fashioned Bertha. So kind, so open-hearted, but still a child inside.

Mrs. Ross confided in me that Bertha takes the frights and spooks of All Hallows' Eve seriously — even more so than the neighborhood children. Children being children, they realized this some time ago, and each year, they make Bertha a victim of their tricks. The four Cary girls live in the house behind the Rosses, and the nasty little cherubs descended upon Bertha, screeching like banshees and dousing her with flour. When a little of it spilled on me, you ought to have seen how apologetic they were amidst howling giggles at the sight of a ghost-white Bertha! And it was not only the children. Later at the party,

Sammy Desmond put the arm of a skeleton around Bertha's shoulders. She almost fell down in a dead faint!

Laura and Mary planned a delightful gathering for us near the pier, unlike any party we have in San Francisco. There was no three-piece band playing softly in the background, no waltzes, no punch and delicate cakes, and no quiet and polite conversation. Everything was loud and jolly. We bobbed for apples and played other games, some of which Papa and perhaps even you would frown upon. Selma, who is the pluckiest and least polished belle, thought up a game she called Ladies Choice. We ladies gathered in the center of a circle with our eyes covered, the young men with their backs to us. We rushed around like chickens, and when a whistle blew, we touched the back of the nearest man. The music began, and we danced blindfolded with our choice. Oh, you needn't worry — it was all in fun, and the young men here are gentlemen.

Later, my nervousness returned, though I cannot think why. Perhaps it was because, with the winding down of the party, the dank fog returned. Or perhaps it was because of little Flossie and her Phooka.

Sammy Desmond, Chase Huxley, and a few of the other young men charmed the children into help us gather wood for the bonfire and invited the little ragamuffins to roast potatoes and apples with us. Flossie sat with Loretta, Bertha, and I. I could see the poor child was more frightened than Bertha. We thought it was because the boys had been especially rascally that evening at the party, but when we assured her they were more interested in roasting apples than frightening the girls, she cried out, "It's the Phooka, the naughty Phooka!"

"Don't be a little ninny," Loretta chided her. "There is no such thing as a ghost, you know."

The little girl's face remained grave. I put my arm around Flossie and asked her to tell me about the Phooka. Poor child!

How she must have had her share of horrors that night, for she took my hand in hers and pulled me into a knot of trees to tell me.

She had heard of the Phooka from her new friend Maggie. "It's an enormous bird, Miss Carlyle," she said.

"Well, that isn't so scary, is it?" I asked.

Her lovely violet eyes were as wide as stars. It seems Maggie had obliged her by drawing a picture of this giant bird with sharp claws and hooked beak. I suggested this Phooka might be nothing more than a hawk or an eagle, but her tiny hand clutched my arm. "No, no, the Phooka has big, pointed teeth like a saw, and it looks like a mad rooster!"

I knew it was useless to tell her this Phooka was some imaginary creature her friend Maggie had made up, no doubt as a Halloween hoax. When I asked her why she was so afraid of the Phooka, she answered, "It carries you away and you never see your mama and papa again!" The little thing buried her face into my skirt and wept, truly wept.

I realized why the name of this bird sounded familiar to me. Do you recall the book in Papa's library, *A Thousand and One Nights*? During Sinbad's voyages, the roc bird takes him in search of elephants and flies him into the valley of the snakes. The picture of the roc bird looked like Flossie's Phooka. I sat little Flossie on my lap, dried her tears, and explained to her such a bird did not exist outside the pages of the Arabian Nights and she needn't be worried about it carrying her or any other child off, never to be seen again.

I don't mind telling you, Mama, that I felt like a heroine, watching the fear melt from Flossie's little face and skip back to the join the others. But must I choose between being the heroine of my own life or someone else's? I would not have thought such a dilemma possible before I came to Waxwood, but in these three months my eyes have seen beyond our little world on Rincon

Hill, and now I know it is so. I must choose one day, as I cannot have both.

Your loving daughter, Penelope

CHAPTER 14

Waxwood, CA November 9, 1852

*D*earest Mama,
    I've finished Mrs. Stowe's book, and it deeply disturbs me. I see now my previous ignorance was more than shameful — it is wrong! Do you remember Grandmother once complained I wasn't as lively as other young ladies on Rincon Hill, and I complained of how shallow they were? I know why now. They were content to be blissful ignorant whereas I thought I was not.

And yet, was I not guilty of the same shallowness? I was a worse offender because I dared think myself better. Perhaps it was because I took to painting and drawing as none of the other young ladies did, and I was told I had a discerning eye. Such compliments are sure to make one conceited!

I am disconcerted now. I have slept badly since I finished the book, seeing the terrified faces in my dreams. Perhaps I am too excitable for such things, even if they are only words. Only words, perhaps, but they have broken that paradise of blissful ignorance in which I have lived for nineteen years.

I was aching to discuss Mrs. Stowe's book, but the belles were uninterested, and the beaus had moved on to other subjects. Mrs. Ross was astounded when I brought up the subject the other night. I knew by the way Mr. Ross snapped his newspaper back and forth that the subject annoyed him. He kept cutting in whenever I tried to speak of it, telling me of this or that story in the paper as if he were trying to distract me from Mrs. Stowe.

And Bertha, poor, old-fashioned Bertha! She almost worships me now and looks at me with soft eyes, not because I want to discuss what I read, but because I read at all! I asked her once if she had not read books as a child. She answered she had read a book of rhymes but remembers nothing of them. To think her mother's closet is filled with books, all beckoning to her, yet she has not even a fleeting interest in them!

Tonight I asked Mrs. Ross if she could give me another book to read. I could see the alarm on her face, but she did not refuse me. Seeing how distressed I was after Mrs. Stowe's book, she reassured me there were many others just as enlightening and less disquieting to a sensitive young woman.

"Don't become bookish, Penelope," Bertha said. "Oh, the horror!"

Naturally Bertha would make such a plea, as one can hardly imagine a debutante bringing a pile of books with her to a ball or luncheon! But neither you needn't fear. From now on, I intend to read books that soothe my nerves, not excite them.

I have now read one of Miss Austen's stories and it is, as Mrs. Ross assured me, more suited to a young woman. I expected romance and fluff, but you know, Mama, these women writers are wily. They write about the courtships and friendships we know so well on Rincon Hill, embedding harsh critiques of society and even politics in the words.

I'm learning how other women live and forming opinions

about them. Making one's own judgments of people is the first link one must break in the chain of ignorance. It's safer to form judgements of made-up people than of real ones, though some of Miss Austen's ladies are more real than those we know in San Francisco. Mrs. Ross asked me the other day what I thought of *Mansfield Park*, and I said, "Fanny Price rather annoys me." She laughed and asked why. I explained I thought her too agreeable and yielding. "And she makes her cousin Edmund into a martyr when he is just a man like any other."

That made Mr. Ross roar with laughter and say I would have no trouble with any man getting the best of me!

I am impatient to see more of Waxwood. Loretta and I will go to the fish market on Sunday. The young ladies here avoid it because of the scent and coarse people. But Loretta goes now and again, as she sometimes helps a woman named Mrs. Bilge whose husband keeps a stall. She tells me it is great fun, and perhaps I shall see Kate again.

Your loving daughter, Penelope

CHAPTER 15

Waxwood, CA November 14, 1852

*D*earest Mama,
　　　　I cannot say I have not had my adventure in Waxwood!

We had our day at the fish market, Mama. After breakfast, Loretta and I slipped away from the belles and walked down to the pier. We merged with a steady flow of gentlemen and ladies of all sorts. Some wore gingham dresses and cotton suits faded from many years of washing, while others donned the highest silk hats and finest laces, as if they were out for a stroll in Lafayette Park. All carried baskets and boxes as if they intended to catch the fish themselves!

Mrs. Bilge's two eldest girls set up the stall for us so we wouldn't get "so much as a stain on yer fine linens." They were quite happy to trod off to their play and leave us with the fish their brothers had caught early that morning. We could barely keep the flies from diving into the feast, but people around us were wonderfully helpful, providing us with newspapers from their precious supply. One might expect those vying for the same coins at the market to be selfish, but I have never seen such graciousness. When I remarked on the fact, a woman with only a few teeth gave a jovial laugh and said, "'T ain't no use, miss, for we all poor together!" I cannot deny it is so, as much as those of us more fortunate ones born into the mansions of Rincon Hill are all rich together.

We had our share of people ogling the fish with no intention of buying. The Bilge boys caught a few giant salmon, and they were a wonder to see. I brought my sketchbook and. when the crowds moved on, sat myself down on a crate (the toothless woman gave me one of hers) and drew a rather good likeness of the salmon.

I had just finished when a young man approached our stall, peering at me among the tickling flies. I had seen him earlier in the day sauntering around the market, his hands shoved in the narrow pockets of his vest and his watch and chain (old and feeble, but polished as if he took good care of it) swinging like a pendulum from his waistcoat. That watch flashed in people's faces and annoyed them as he passed. I thought no more of him than of the other youths prowling about.

He fell into a small crowd gathered around the last salmon at our table. People began their bargaining. Loretta, with her gentle nature, was hardly up to the task, her face peaked and damp. I made her sit down and took over the bargaining. The war was half-won on our side at fifteen cents for the amiable fish when the young man put his hand on the salmon and declared, "None of you shall have it. It's been promised to me."

I assumed this was nothing more than the impudence of youth and continued with the bargaining. He repeated, "It's been promised to *me*."

I told him he could have it if he had the fifteen cents to pay for it. And the impertinent lad insisted it had been promised to him for nothing!

This made the crowd disperse, howling with laughter. Loretta, recovered from her fatigue, said, "Oh, let him have it, Penelope."

"Penelope?" The boy examined me with his green eyes. "Why, you're nothing like her."

He began quoting from a poem of "the fair, faithful, fidelity of Penelope." I truly had no idea to whom or what he was referring, and I believe the scamp was only trying to distract me from my task. He would not budge an inch, but neither would I. I told him the fish was fifteen cents, and we would take not a penny less, as Mrs. Bilge is a good woman who worked hard and had seven mouths to feed.

The brazen boy put his cap to one side, and scoffed, "Seven mouths? I have twenty-two!"

Of course I didn't believe him for a moment. "That is quite a large family for such a boy," said I.

"I never said they were family," he answered.

I suggested he leave at once and pointed out the two lawmen a short distance away. He continued to rattle on about his twenty-two mouths to feed. Loretta, with her soft heart, inquired about this so-called family, and he began describing them, including several "women posing for posterity."

Loretta pulled me aside and told me she thought he must be from Brandywine. I had heard of the place from the Belles and their beaus: an art colony isolated in the wax wood forest, its people lovers of solitude.

The brash boy looked at me with sly eyes and remarked I had an interesting face and might I oblige him by coming to pose for him one day?

The insufferable rascal! "I'm a *lady*," I said.

"Oh, we have a few of those," he said. "They're not as lofty as you in their thinking, though."

"More's the pity they are obviously less willing to teach manners to young boys like you!" I retorted.

All at once, he turned from a boy to a man. He bowed and introduced himself as Evan Jones and apologized for his scampish behavior. "I agree it was most undignified of me," he said. "But I'm not a boy, miss. I turned twenty-four last month."

"Twenty-four!" I had taken his smooth face and wandering eyes as not much older than seventeen.

"May I ask how old you are?"

"You may not!"

"Very well, Miss Penelope." He stepped back. "'One shade the more, one ray the less, Had half impaired the nameless grace…'"

I told him he would not sway me to give him the salmon with pretty words. He said they were not his but Lord Byron's. "Regardless," I said, "they will not sway me."

Loretta took me aside again and with her sweet charity, convinced me we could not deny the young man the salmon if he could give us at least a dime for it, as it was late and stalls were folding up to go home. Her common sense melted my temper, and I went back to Mr. Jones with this condensation. But would you believe the scoundrel would have none of it? He kept insisting Mrs. Bilge promised him the fish for nothing, and he would not pay one cent for it.

I told him to take the salmon and go away. He tipped his hat in thanks and then glanced at me with his half-winking eyes, saying he gave me credit for having more spirit than most *ladies* he knew, in spite of my haughtiness. "I think we shall meet soon," he concluded.

I may tell you, Mama, I have no intention of ever seeing the scamp again. But now that I have calmed down, I am less inclined to judge his character so harshly. Perhaps it was his duty toward the twenty-two people in his "family" that made him so stubborn. There is virtue in such obstinacy.

Your loving daughter, Penelope

CHAPTER 16

Waxwood, CA December 3, 1852

*D*earest Mama,
 I found out a little more about Mr. Evan Jones. He lives in Brandywine with his sister and niece and comes to town quite often

The belles insist the artist are outcasts, but Loretta assured me they are above reproach, simply preferring to be left alone. She seemed afraid Mr. Jones may try to persuade me to join the colony. Of course, the idea is preposterous. San Francisco is where I belong, though for the time being, I am content here in Waxwood.

Today Mrs. Ross gave a dinner party, and we all had to help. Mrs. Batt was moaning over the burnt roast, so Mrs. Ross asked Bertha and I to fetch a turkey from the butcher's. Mr. Knowles had sold his last fowl before we arrived but, with the simple altruism so typical of these coastal people, he closed his shop, hitched his wagon, and rode us out to a farmer he knew who kept chickens and turkeys whom, he assured us, would be glad to sell us one for our Friday feast.

The trip itself was well worth it. The scenery laid out in as many variations of green as you can imagine. Mr. Knowles seemed proud of my awe . He looks upon me as a kind of ambassador and intends I should return to San Francisco raving about their fair little town. "Our side of the bay mightn't be as grand as yours, but our greenery ain't nothin' to sniff at!" he insisted.

Who do you suppose was at the Goodwin farm, leaning against the fence in that sauntering pose? That swine Mr. Jones! And would you believe, Mama, he was using the same deceptive methods to get Mr. Goodwin to give him a turkey as he had the salmon? Mr. Goodwin told him he would let his turkey Matilda go for eleven cents and no less, and the rascal insisted Mrs. Goodwin had promised it to him for nothing.

Mr. Jones recognized me and greeted me with a familiarity that appalled Bertha. After warning Mr. Jones not to give us any trouble, Mr. Goodwin insisted his wife wouldn't have made such a promise as they had six children, "God bless 'em all."

"That is nothing to Mr. Jones," I scoffed. "*He* has twenty-two!"

Mr. Jones seemed delighted. "Blessed be, the lady has far better humor today! And she is looking far prettier too."

The young man's impertinence irked me from the first, and now he was throwing insolent compliments my way! But, eager to fulfill Mr. Ross' prophecy, I vowed not to allow this scamp to get the best of me. I offered Mr. Goodwin fifteen cents for Matilda, and he gave a deep sigh of gratitude. Mr. Jones kept insisting Mrs. Goodwin had promised it to him, and I had no right to buy it. "I'm sure Miss Penelope does not doubt my rectitude," he said.

"I believe your rectitude is as reliable as it was at the fish market," I answered. "And you know what I thought of that!" This put Bertha in one of her flutters. Old-fashioned Bertha, frightened even to speak to a young man!

The farmer laughed and disappeared into the barn with Mr. Knowles. Mr. Jones leaned against the gate, his hands in his pockets. His scrutinizing eyes made me draw my shawl closer to me. I asked him why he was watching me. The brash devil did not deny it, and Bertha's agitation reached its peak as she accused him of being "an improper thing."

Mr. Jones took out a handkerchief and wiped his face with it. He apologized to us both in a way that did not lack sincerity. He told me he had seen me on the pier with my sketchbook, and we got into a conversation about my drawing. He was genuinely interested, his manner serious and pleasant. He said he should like to draw me as Tatiana, the queen of the fairies.

"A faithless queen," I reminded him.

"Only in Oberon's imagination," he countered.

Mr. Goodwin and Mr. Knowles came back, each dragging a turkey behind them. Mr. Jones' earnest manner disappeared, and he grabbed Matilda and rushed off with her. Mr. Goodwin ran after him, but in vain. We could hear Matilda's squawks die out as the impish boy disappeared.

Seeing the gloomy look on Mr. Goodwin's face, I flung open my handbag and handed him three dimes for both turkeys.

All the way back to town, Bertha and Mr. Knowles commended me on my generosity. To tell the truth, Mama, I did it as much for Mr. Jones and his "family" as for Mr. Goodwin's. I cannot say why.

Your loving daughter, Penelope

CHAPTER 17

Waxwood CA December 14, 1852

*D*earest Mama,

I no longer see myself as merely a debutante. Since my meeting with Evan Jones, I have thought quite a lot about Brandywine. Though I would never go off to live with the bohemians, everyone here sees me as an artist.

I enjoy reading the books Mrs. Ross gives me, but they are no longer enough. I must *do* more. What good is it to be virtuous and kind so that one may take one's place in heaven if one has nothing to show for one's life when one gets there?

I have seen Evan Jones again. I wonder I ever thought him a rascal and a devious swine, for his conduct today was quite agreeable. Mr. Jones does not come from some backwoods tribe but was raised to be virtuous and respectable. He is as solid as any of the young men working for Papa and a good deal more compassionate.

When I sketch now, I think often of Miss Gilbert. In between those lessons of the gentile talents suitable for a lady were gleams of wisdom. She was more suited to be a professor than a governess and might have made a fine one, had she been a man. She forced me to notice the finer details in life. "Pay attention, child, to the finer details," she used to say. "They contain the greatest lessons of the world."

I search for those finer details: the cluster of grass in the water, the silver lines on a rock, the stump bobbing out of tune with the bay. I languish on these details in my drawings, and then I draw them again and again. It is madness, perhaps, but one's follies may sometimes lead to enlightenment.

This morning I went to the outer edge of the pier. A yellow boathouse and dilapidated boat stand half buried in the bay. A puffin waddled across the boathouse floor. The bird jumped onto shore and collapsed on the rocks. Its lolling head and somber eyes intrigued me, so I made a sketch. Just as I had started on the second one, Mr. Jones appeared in the distance, completely swathed in flannel. As he came closer, he peered at me in the way he had at the fish market and the farm.

"Good morning, Miss Carlyle." It was the first time he addressed me in the proper way.

He proceeded to thank me for paying for Matilda. He admitted it was reprehensible to steal a turkey, but he did not do it for a lark. The children in the colony needed meat, and although people in town were generous, he felt ashamed coming to them with his hands out. His cheeks flushed as he added, "Perhaps I'm too young a provider for twenty-two people, but I have taken on the task of my own free will."

I rewarded his frankness by asking him to call me Penelope, as I felt sure you would advise me to do so, Mama. He growled, "How I despise that name!" Remembering what he told me, I asked, "Is the name of a fair and faithful wife so detestable?" He answered, "It is ill-suited for you." He explained it was not that he believed I lacked fairness and faithfulness, but that these were only outward qualities. He picked up my sketchbook and added, "Anyone who can draw with such painstaking care must have more to her than that."

I don't think Bertha or Laura or Selma or even Loretta would have taken this as a compliment. They would have found a young man who made such presumptions of character impertinent. But I recognized he was genuinely alluding to something more in my favor.

I could not contain my curiosity and asked him what name he would give me instead. He studied me for a moment, and I felt a little unsettled by his glaring eyes. He answered, "Grace."

I had been hoping for something more majestic, like Philomena or Gertrude. I did not expect him to choose a name so delicate it wilts the moment it leaves one's lips.

I asked him if it was because I had "one shade more, one ray less," and he seemed pleased I remembered Byron. He admitted he had done me a disservice that day, as perhaps I was a nameless grace but hardly without unique shades and rays.

He asked to see my sketches. I agreed, but his scrutiny of them made me quite self-conscious. He asked me why I drew so many fish. I told him I found the creatures spellbinding. "They remind me of Tiresias," I added. "Do you think that's silly? "

He answered, "Not silly, but one must move beyond still-life if one is to be a serious artist." He asked why I don't draw people or landscapes. "I can never seem to capture the inequities of the human face or the glories of Mother Nature," I said.

"Ah, but have you really tried?" he challenged me. I admitted I had never really given it an earnest effort. He spoke of releasing the courage and inhibitions necessary to experiment with art and hinted if I came to the colony, I would see for myself. This I have little desire to do, though it would be an adventure.

He added, "If you'll pardon my saying so, I do not feel your soul is free."

I could not be angry at him, for have I not been saying as

much to you in my letters? How can one be free when one has been brought up not to veer from one's path?

He rose and declared, "Your little Tiresias will never liberate your soul, Grace."

I want to do as he suggests, but I scarcely know how. Don't misunderstand, Mama, I am *not* unhappy. But one may be happy and discontented if one's path has come to a halt, and one knows just beyond the trees lays another one cannot reach.

Your loving daughter, Penelope

CHAPTER 18

Waxwood, CA December 25, 1852

*D*earest Mama,

I wish you and Papa a Merry Christmas with all my heart and joy. I miss you both. I miss Mrs. Dale's roast duck and apple pie and caramel ices and the tree reigning over us in the parlor with the little angle perched on top, bowing her head in grace.

I was unabashedly childish when, after breakfast, we opened our gifts. Loretta and her family arrived with a pitcher of eggnog. Flossie, still at the age where Christmas delights her imagination, hung over everyone's shoulder as they opened their presents.

The Rosses were very generous. I received my first set of pastels! I wish you and Papa could have seen my face when I opened the box and beheld the beautiful colors in their velvet beds. I have been trying to take Evan's advice and draw faces, but they look more like marble statues than flesh and blood. Perhaps the pastels will improve them.

I also received a lovely fan of real peacock feathers from Bertha, and Loretta gave me two books of poetry, including those lovely Portuguese verses from Mrs. Barrett Browning. I read through them once, and they are so lovely, Mama! I will send the book to you in the next post so you may enjoy them too.

After all the presents had been opened, we noticed one in back of the tree that had no name. We thought at first the children were playing a joke, but they swore they had never seen it. When Mr. Ross examined it, he discovered the name "Grace" faintly scrawled in the corner. My face warmed as I admitted it was for me. Naturally they were curious as to who had sent it to me and why it was addressed to "Grace".

When Mrs. Ross questioned the servants, Tillie admitted a "right amiable gentleman" had given her the package, claiming to be a friend of the family. Of course I knew who she meant, but kept silent as the others contemplated which of the beaus had left the gift. Mr. Potter guessed it was the bashful Mr. Huxley while Mr. Ross sang praises for Mr. Caselton, in whom, he suspected, "still waters run deep."

"We won't know until Penelope opens it, will we?" Mrs. Ross asked.

"Oh, Penelope, you must, you must!" Bertha said, and the children added their pleas.

I had the modesty (or perhaps the selfishness) to wish to open the gift privately, but I couldn't disappoint those anxious faces. I unwrapped the paper, and a card fell out, which I quickly hid in my pocket. Evan had done a drawing of me that bore my likeness in vibrant colors and vivid lines, probably with pastels, not unlike those I had just received. The frame in which the picture lay is like nothing I've ever seen. It is engraved with fluted branches, and swans rest in the sun while frogs eye flies with roguish gazes as if about to eat them.

Everyone looked over my shoulder, gasping and admiring. Mr. Ross declared he never would have guessed Mr. Caselton had such a deft hand, and Mrs. Ross conceded he had captured my "untarnished loveliness."

And yet, Mama, the more I gazed at the face staring back at me, the more I felt I were looking into the face of a stranger. The portrait is of a debutante with cinnamon hair and smooth skin, wearing a peach dress heaped with frills such as I might wear. She looks so supplicating and scrumptious, one could put her in a glass case!

Had not Evan told me he saw more than fairness and faithfulness in me? Had he not conceded to my unique shades and rays? But here was this mendacious version of myself drawn by his own hand.

Mr. Potter, who can be rough, suddenly exclaimed, "I shouldn't be surprised if the young man were looking for an opportunity to give away that frame, it's so awful!"

It was an unkind thing to say, as the frame, though gaudy, is clearly valuable. How many salmon and Matildas could that frame bring for those twenty-two hungry people? I surmised it must be a Jones family heirloom, and yet, he had given it to me.

Oh, Mama, I was so deeply touched. Tears sprang into my eyes, and I retreated to the veranda for some fresh air. I still had the note in my pocket. The paper had been used many times, showing signs of fading, but I managed to read Evan's words:

Please accept this gift as a small token of our friendship. I beg to apologize if I insulted you with my presumptuousness. I have a reckless nature that has more than once led me into trouble. I hope the portrait meets with your approval.

I invite you to come to Brandywine and see it for yourself. You must have heard rumors about us, and though I care nothing for what others think, I don't want you to think ill of us. I consider you one of us in spirit.

Would you come to tea at five o'clock on the 29th? I assure you, it will be a thoroughly proper tea with my sister and niece in attendance, our best china, and Ebba's lemon teacakes.

Perhaps you will indulge me further by bringing your sketchbook as I am eager to see how you have progressed since our last meeting.

Ebba also wants to meet you. She is more talented than I, and I'm sure you'll enjoy seeing her sculptures.

You may ask anyone in town how to get to the colony. It is not a difficult or unpleasant journey. I would offer to come and escort you, but I am loath to leave my sister just now.

Your humble servant, Evan Jones

A lovely invitation and quite sincere, don't you think, Mama? I am madly curious to see the colony. But it frightens me too, like an invitation to walk into a dream without the promise of coming out again.

Your loving daughter, Penelope

CHAPTER 19

Waxwood, CA December 29, 1852

Dearest Mama,
Do you remember how Papa would wave a finger at me when I was a child and say, "Take care, curiosity killed the cat." I felt a little like that cat today.

I asked the Rosses for their advice regarding Evan's invitation. Mr. Ross asked many questions about my acquaintance with Evan and agreed the young man's intentions appeared honorable. Mrs. Ross was at first hesitant, more for propriety's sake than anything else. She conceded it would be honorable to accept Evan's invitation so long as his sister and niece were there. She suggested she come with me, insisting Evan would hardly expect a young lady to attend a tea with people she hardly knew without a chaperone if he were as familiar with social etiquette as he implied. But I preferred to go alone, and I am sure he prefers it, or he wouldn't have made such a point of telling me his sister and niece would be there.

Already at three I was dressed in my green silk and taffeta with the rose-colored bows. I felt like a cooked goose drowning in too much gravy. I don't believe I have ever been so anxious about a tea in my life.

Bertha insisted on seeing me to the pier where the ferry would take me to the colony. She tried to make me feel more at ease by relating some little quarrel between Selma and Patricia over Lem Austin. I hardly listened to that tweeting voice as I was too preoccupied with trying to calm myself.

I was frightened when the ferry let me off in a bald wilderness, but I determined to follow through on this adventure, and found the narrow path Mr. Ross had drawn for me. It did not take me long to reach the colony, and the way was, as Evan promised, pleasant. I finally saw the fascinating wax wood trees, their bark glistening a million colors in the sun, along with the scarlet redwoods I love so much. In a girlish whimsy, I gathered a little bouquet of wild violets and orange poppies to give Evan's little niece.

I don't know what I expected. I suppose I had visions of squalid, mud-packed shanties hidden among the trees. Brandywine is nothing of the kind. Why, it's almost like a tiny village! The houses are slight but have proper roofs and small gardens. The gate surrounding it is a huddle of wood panels painted by the artists of the colony, intended to let people in rather than keep them out.

Evan was waiting for me and walked me to his house. We passed people sitting in their gardens, in the walkway and even in the middle of the road! It is at that hour of the day, Evan explained, when many like to work in the open air. A few exchanged words with him, eyeing my formal attire with some amusement. When he told them I was an artist, they welcomed me with friendly smiles.

Ebba is four or five years older than Evan though her manner is more mature. She has a regal pose of one who has taken responsibility from a young age, but she is far from rigid or unpleasant. In fact, there was a nimbleness about her, as if she may fly away at any moment. She laughed often and skipped around. singing whenever her daughter came in from her play in the garden. What inquisitive eyes Verina has! She is one who will look upon people as a stone goddess looks upon her observers, intent on wringing mortality out of them.

Evan told me Ebba was very gifted, and he was right. She is inspired by Greek and Roman figures, mostly the women, but makes something entirely different of them. My favorite is the Demeter and Persephone. Demeter is bewitching, and Persephone is hardly the surrendering angel one sees in Bernini's figure. In Ebba's hands, she looks as if she were going to shoot Hades in the belly!

She was quite generous with her praise of my sketches, telling me I made almost mystical creatures of the fish. Oh, the joy of having one who understands one's art!

Evan was exuberant over my progress. "You have taken it more seriously," he said. But perhaps what gratified me the most was when Evan thrust my sketchbook at several people who came by. They examined the fish and were rather pleased with them, agreeing I had transformed those illusive creatures into noteworthy subjects. When they went away, smiling and nodding, I felt giddy with relief and gratitude.

As we walked back to the gate, Evan took my arm and asked me if I was now ready to embrace courage and experimentation. I admitted I could in a community of like-minded people. Yes, I could fly like a bird in Brandywine!

Your loving daughter, Penelope

CHAPTER 20

Brandywine, Waxwood, CA February 7, 1853

*D*earest Mama,
    I know Mrs. Ross has written you, but I wanted to write you myself when I was ready.

I am thriving. I have no more nervous attacks, and I am more fit than I've ever been. That is because I have been living in Brandywine for three weeks.

A few days after my visit with the Joneses, Evan came to see me and asked me to come stay with him and Ebba at the colony as their guest.

He told me how he had come there in the first place. He did not start out drawing portraits. He wanted to put his artistic skills to use expanding and building San Francisco, as he loved it as much as Papa does. When he was sixteen, a friend of his great-aunt obtained an apprenticeship for him in an architectural firm. The more he worked there, the more the buildings he loved became like prison cells. "My intellect appreciated their symmetry," he said. "But my heart longed for something more liberating."

He stayed on for the sake of the man who had generously offered him a way out of the pious life with his great-aunt. The firm added another partner, a middle-aged man named Mr. Sprout. One Sunday, Evan came to the office, and Mr. Sprout was there. He saw Evan arranging some works he had done hidden in the workroom. "He said to me? 'Leave here and seek your fortune, even if it is a small one. You'll have the comfort of knowing your hand touched the stars even for a brief time.'" And then Mr. Sprout told Evan about Brandywine.

Perhaps it was in the back of my mind to go there all along, Mama. The past year I have gone through the motions, doing all you told me was right for a young woman such as myself to do. Those encouraging words I received regarding my sketches at Brandywine invigorated me in a way no party or ball ever could. Perhaps all along my spirit has been with that little place among the wax wood trees.

I cannot explain it better than this: if I am to come back to you and Papa and Rincon Hill a woman alive, I must be free for a time. Call it an adventure or a lark or a fling, if you wish. But I must try to touch the stars for at least a little while.

Your loving daughter, Penelope

P.S. - YOU SEE I sign my letter with the name Evan gave me. I have not shed Penelope entirely, but I would like to try being Grace for a while. — GC

CHAPTER 21

Brandywine, Waxwood, CA March 18, 1853

*D*earest Mama,
    I have now been in Brandywine a few months, and I feel sure my heart has guided me wisely. You will see, I'll come back to the city a woman you and Papa can be proud of. My limbs are lighter, my movements easier, and my nerves steadier.

I am getting to know the colony. People here are very favorable. They are not bohemians or wayfarers as you feared, Mama. They are fine people with fine manners and morals. Many attend the church in Waxwood, and some go to the synagogue in Placo, a nearby town. People often come after dinner to visit with us in the garden, bearing gifts like wild blueberries from the woods or a clothespin doll for Verina. They talk about art and life in ways we on Rincon Hill never do.

Many of the artists take advantage of the beautiful landscape for their work, though for their bread and butter. People flock to Waxwood from the cities to breathe in the clean air and the sea, and they wish to take the memory of the serene bay with them so they may gaze upon it hanging in their parlors or bedrooms when they are back in the city. The artists, then, take advantage of this and go into town to sell their paintings or drawings.

It's not that they find the landscape displeasing, but they dislike these bland views favored by the tourists. Frank, who lives at the other end of the circle here, calls it "the sacrifice of communication for the masses." Think of a wide plain, Mama. Its vastness may look impressive in a painting hanging on a parlor wall, but it could be any plain from anywhere in the country. There is nothing that makes it uniquely brilliant.

I was impatient to practice what they preach, but I let my nerves to get the better of me until yesterday. I asked Evan to take me to the woods. I have taken walks there on my own, but he took me to a particularly flat land that was like a forest of castles with wax wood and redwood trees and clover ground. It reminded me of that night we went to see *A Midsummer Night's Dream*, and I was so fascinated by the scenery with the fairies sparkling under the gaslights. I told Evan, "I see Titania and the fairies playing here."

He laughed, but then became serious when he put the sketch-book in my lap and directed me to draw the fairies singing Titania to sleep as I imagined them in this place. I felt like a child playing in the sand as I did what he asked. The fairy queen looked like Verina.

We must have spent hours working side by side without saying a word to each other. There is something about the unflagging concentration of two people at work that give vigor to both parties. I didn't realize the time until I heard in the distance Verina and her mother playing and laughing. Their floating laughter was like the scent of apples. Perfect specimens of visiting fairies!

Evan was pleased with my work, remarking of how I could draw child-like creatures with beautiful innocence. It reminded me of Halloween, but now I felt none of the ambivalence I felt then. As an artist, I am the heroine of my own story.

Ebba and Verina emerged from the bushes with baskets on their arms. Verina ran to me and spilled hers into my lap. The blackberries had the most heavenly sweetness, Mama. Ebba told me they are not native to the area, but some seeds had mysteriously flourished. Perhaps I shall be like that — the wild berry that flourishes.

I see what Evan means now when he said my fish were frozen subjects. The little Tiresias still fascinate me, but I look at the redfish I drew and see a sea gryphon with blood scales and gold teeth that I never want to draw again.

Your loving daughter, Grace

CHAPTER 22

Brandywine, Waxwood, CA May 9, 1853

*D*earest Mama,

I'm happy Papa is much better. Don't you think it wise he agreed to give up some of his business activities? I am glad Mr. Alderdice made Papa see it would be best for him to visit downtown only a few days during the week. I personally find the young man a little too persuasive. Is he really considering coming to Waxwood for the summer? I cannot imagine him enjoying a stroll on the pier or croquet with the belles and their beaus. I know they would find him coarse and cold.

My faith in people's kindness has grown since I came to the colony. There is nothing artificial or empty about the benevolence here. The artists give generously of their time and attention.

I draw most of the time, but I continue reading, as I find words as comforting as pictures. Mrs. Ross chooses my books for me and sends them up with Loretta, who has become a frequent visitor.

Verina, I have mentioned, is an inquisitive child. Every time Loretta unwraps the paper from the packages Mrs. Ross sends me, the little girl watches, her eyes large as if wanting to devour them. My heart goes out to her, for I felt the same way last year when I watched Mrs. Ross settling in with her books. I felt as if I were missing something very important.

Today we had no visitors. A stretch of stars appeared like little lanterns in the night sky. Evan took out his pipe and Ebba tended to her darning, which she does well. I settled down with Elizabeth Gaskell's *Ruth*. I became engrossed in the novel for a time until I realized Verina was standing before me.

I don't think she can read very well, Mama. I dislike saying so, but I believe her mother has neglected her education. I have never seen a schoolbook around the house. I asked Evan about this once, but he only said, "She is a bright child, and her little mind explores everything, which is far better than any book learning."

I took her to my lap and suggested we read together The little girl shot her mother a look, the small brows knitting together. Seeing no objection, she insisted I tell her the story. Evan scolded her for being coarse, but I understood why she would not read with me. It's hardly pleasant when one reads poorly. I told her as much as I knew about the character of Ruth. Verina asked, "Did Ruth and Mr. Bellingham marry?" I tried to skirt the question, explaining Mr. Bellingham had to go away with his mother. Verina inquired why they did not get married before he went away (I told you she's an inquisitive child.) That, Mama, is a more sordid part of the story which I held back. I said they knew their love would keep until he returned.

Ebba leapt up and accused me of filling the girl's head with lies about love and devotion. "Why don't you tell her Mr.

Bellingham abandons Ruth?" she screamed. "Why don't you tell her he leaves her with child?"

I cringed at the fire in her eyes. Poor Verina whimpered as she slid off my lap and hid behind some bushes. Evan came to my defense, insisting there was no reason to be angry with me for telling Verina a harmless story. Ebba insisted it was not harmless, as lies only led to sorrow and pain. She burst into tears and ran into the house, Verina sobbing at her heels.

Evan's face was red with shame. "She's been much deceived in love," he lamented. "A wounded heart strives to keep other hearts from being wounded." I asked if he felt like his sister about love. He took my hand and assured me they were not. I was relieved to hear this, as Evan and I have grown closer and I should hate to think him cynical about love and affection.

Ebba retreated to her studio and did not even come out for dinner. I did not expect to see her until the morning, but as I was preparing for bed, she came in and offered to brush my hair. She assured me I had no cause to beg her forgiveness. "I was like Ruth once," she confessed.

She told me the story of her betrayal. He had been a young lawyer who acquainted with the same man who had seen to Evan's education. He had pretty words, she said, just like Mr. Bellingham, and a pretty way about him. He made promises like Mr. Bellingham. She ran away with him, but he soon tired of her. "He went for a walk one morning and never came back."

As she spoke, she yanked at my hair harder and harder as if she were trying to release the pain of it. I told her my head was splitting, but she wouldn't stop. Evan appeared at the doorway and, seeing what she was doing, grabbed the brush from her hand. My hand flew to my head. I felt a small bald spot in the back. Ebba put her hands to her face, and her mouth opened to let out the most frightening screech I have ever heard. Evan caught her in time as she collapsed into his arms, wailing and screeching as if some devil possessed her. He stayed with her in her studio until she fell to sleep.

It saddens me how a woman's faith in love can be damaged. Perhaps we are too eagerly pushed into men's arms without being taught to question whether they deserve our faith, and trust. I know only one man who is deserving of those precious gifts.

Your loving daughter, Grace

CHAPTER 23

Brandywine, Waxwood, CA June 3, 1853

*D*earest Mama,

  I hope I said nothing in my last letter to frighten you or make you think there was anything improper between Evan and I. We are good friends, but that should not worry you in the least. He is not a Waxwood beau, nor a Rincon Hill gentleman, but he is respectable and strives to please me in every way.

  I know Mr. Alderdice is in Waxwood, as I have already seen him. He was on the pier when Evan and I went down to do some sketching. He behaved very much like a gentleman, though I cannot deny he always reminds me of a wooden soldier. He asked me many questions about my activities here in Waxwood, looking to Evan for confirmation, which irked me to no end. Evan only nodded in reply.

  I know you and Papa have never understood why I dislike Mr. Alderdice. I'm sure he has a fine mind and sound business judgment. I don't doubt he will rise quickly in the ranks of Carlyle

Shipping. I concede he has pleasant manners without the hauteur of some social-climbing young men I have met, and his countenance is not unpleasing. Indeed, if one were to examine Mr. Alderdice under a glass, one would find nothing wrong with him. And yet he disturbs me. I think him cool and impersonal, but more than that, there is a drive in him that knows no boundaries.

Perhaps you will understand better if I tell you about a certain incident that occurred a few days after we met at the pier. I received a note from Bertha insisting she had something very urgent to discuss with me and asked me to come to tea. I naturally obliged, as I would never deny Bertha anything. The "something urgent" was entirely a fiction. Bertha wasn't even at home when I arrived! When Tillie showed me into the parlor (giggling inside her apron), I found Mr. Alderdice sitting very erect and anxious on the couch.

He admitted it was not Bertha who invited me to tea but himself. I scolded him for taking advantage of one of the best souls on earth (poor, innocent Bertha) to aid in this deception, and I was ready to leave, despite my promise to be civil to him.

Mr. Alderdice implored me to stay. He insisted he had not ill-used Bertha, as she had willingly written the note, knowing I would not come if he had sent it himself (which is true). He assured me it was not a ruse, as he had "important business" to discuss with me. As he had behaved in this dishonest manner to insure I would come, I accepted the cup of tea Tillie gave me with a approving smile. How the girl has romantic notions!

He asked me if I were enjoying myself in "the wilds." I asked, "Is that why you've come to Waxwood, Mr. Alderdice, to explore 'the wilds'?" He mumbled something about wanting to come up to Waxwood for some time, as he had heard the fishing was superb. I did not believe him and told him so, hinting he had come to spy on me. Mr. Alderdice smiled as I've never seen him smile before. His smiles have always been condescending, but this one was rather artless. "You are honest, Miss Carlyle," he said. "A quality I admire greatly." He affirmed to my suspicions.

I have said he is devious, and does this not prove it?

I became enraged, not so much by his impertinence, but by the delight he took in admitting it. I could hardly contain myself as I rose and said, "I don't think my father will be very pleased when he hears about it." He insisted Papa was worried about me and "this colony business." Mama, you have shown Papa my letters. It would have been more prudent not to have done so, as there is much he does not understand about young women.

I assured Mr. Alderdice I was not naïve and knew how to avoid rogues and rascals. He remarked that rogues and rascals were one thing, as their evil was transparent, but one could never be sure of the blackguards who paraded as gentlemen. "I fear you have put yourself in the path of such a man," he said. He noticed how fond I was of Mr. Jones and he of me. He reminded me of the biblical words: *Beware of false prophets, which come to you in sheep's clothing, but inwardly they are ravening wolves.*

The impudence of the man! To insinuate Evan was a blackguard and his regard for me was improper! "Mr. Jones may be a false prophet or a wolf in sheep's clothing." He continued. "I don't know which."

"But you assume he is one or the other?" I railed. "You are wrong, sir. He is neither. He is a kind and generous man."

"I beg to explain myself, Miss Carlyle," he said. He told me he and Evan had known one another as boys, though they had not been friends. I understand then why Evan was so silent when we first met Mr. Alderdice on the pier, though why he did not tell me, I don't know.

"I know him well enough to know he can be a fiend," Mr. Alderdice concluded.

I know it was hardly ladylike, but I snatched my hat and gloves and bid him an icy "good day." He apologized and offered me his hand. I shook it for Papa's sake. And then he said something quite peculiar, Mama. He said, "I am your friend, Miss Carlyle. Should you ever need anything, you may come to me, and I will help you."

Despite his calculating nature, I believe he meant what he said. But I will never need his friendship or his help.

Your loving daughter, Grace

CHAPTER 24

Brandywine, Waxwood, CA June 25, 1853

*D*earest Mama,

Evan avoids going into town now. The colony likes to send him on their errands, as his boyish charm melts the most ice-hearted merchant. But lately he comes up with one excuse after another to keep from going down the hill. I suspect he is trying to avoid Mr. Alderdice. I cannot blame him.

Today was Loretta's twentieth birthday, and Ebba and I persuaded him to come with us to her party. The Potter garden is a lovely place with the summer roses blooming and the gazebo with the vine leaves falling on our heads like raindrops. Evan chatted expertly with Mr. Potter about its architecture. His years as an apprentice in San Francisco have stayed with him.

Little Flossie took a liking to Verina and brought out the shy thing, pulling her into the house to show her all her lovely toys and dresses. The pained look on Ebba's face as she watched her daughter trot after Loretta's sister told a great deal about being unable to give her daughter the fine things Mrs. Potter gave Flossie. As much as she adores Brandywine, I cannot help but feel she wishes Verina to leave it one day and seek a life apart from that sheltering among the wax wood trees.

Mr. Alderdice was there as well. I have seen him in town several times since our tea. He is always polite, and always ends with a reminder of what he said to me at the tea. Some of the belles flirt with him, especially Laura. Loretta told me she and Selma have been rivals since they were children, and now that Selma is getting married, she is anxious to follow.

I don't deny Mr. Alderdice cuts a romantic figure with his well-tailored suits and calm demeanor. But at the party, he looked pompous and over-dressed with his stiff collar and his walking stick. Imagine, a young man not even thirty with a walking stick!

Evan noticed this too, and I am ashamed to admit, he took advantage of it in the most unkind way. He remarked within Mr. Alderdice's hearing how it was a pity some people's ill manners could cast an ill wind upon a festive occasion. "They ought to leave and let others enjoy themselves in peace."

I did not like him gloating over someone else's discomfort, Mama. I reminded him parties were filled with frivolity and it was natural those with a more serious nature would not enjoy them. Mr. Alderdice commended me, adding. "Miss Carlyle and I clearly prefer honesty over frippery. We had a lively conversation about this at tea the other day."

"Tea?" Evan's face flushed and his eyes burned.

"Certainly," Mr. Alderdice answered. "I invited Miss Carlyle to tea, which the Rosses kindly allowed. Did she not tell you about it?"

He bowed stiffly to Mr. Alderdice and pulled me into the empty gazebo. His voice rang with indignation as he demanded to know why I had not told him it was Mr. Alderdice with whom I had had tea and not Bertha. I assured him I had accepted only because Papa expected it of me. This calmed him enough to return to the party.

A little later, when we gathered around Loretta to cut the birthday cake, my eye fell on Mr. Alderdice, standing apart from the others. I understood his feelings, as Waxwood, though not unfriendly, has its petty notions of society just as we do in the city. He is an outsider in this social circle, as I am now, though I cannot fathom why this should be, since he never makes a false step and has a gift for conversation when he chooses.

When Loretta gave me a piece of the birthday cake, I gave it to him. He accepted the plate, but his eyes cast down so I could not see their faded blue. Perhaps this sealed the friendship he had offered me as blood wounds seal children's solemn oath to be true to one another.

Verina pranced up and showed her mother a doll Flossie had given her. It was a sweet thing with a china head and red shoes. Loretta told me a local woman made it, and Flossie adored it when she was younger. It moved me that the child would give such a beloved toy to Verina.

Ebba snatched it away and, cradling it in her arms, smiled and murmuring, "Sleep now, little Ebba, sleep." She recited a rhyme about Mary slaughtering a lamb under a full moon, then threw the doll into the punch bowl. Verina ran screaming from the garden. We calmed her mother with a little whiskey, but, naturally, it was impossible for us to stay after that.

Before we left, Mr. Alderdice took me aside and implored me to leave the colony. "Those people are irrational, and I fear they will influence you." I insisted he did not know these people as I did, that they were sometimes eccentric but always harmless. "This is far more than eccentricity," he answered. "Ask Mr. Jones about his mother."

On the ferry home, Ebba and Verina dozed while Evan and I took a turn around the deck. I could not stop thinking of what Mr. Alderdice had said. I did not want to ask, but I could not keep still. To my surprise, my question did not offend Evan. He admitted his father died of fever, as he had told me, but as for his mother, "brain fever struck her most severely." He admitted she had had outbursts like Ebba, and they had to place her in an asylum. He wept like a little boy as he told me, Mama. Oh, how my heart wept too, sobbing along with his boyish broken heart!

Your loving daughter, Grace

CHAPTER 25

Brandywine, Waxwood, CA July 4, 1853

earest Mama,

Though I miss the excitement of San Francisco, Waxwood did not deprive us of the day's festivities. The town council holds a community picnic every year, and when the sun goes down, they arrange for rockets and fire balloons on the pier. Everyone in town, the artists attend.

Evan has his vanities as much as I have mine, as he fussed over his suit, brushing the vest of every particle of dust and eyeing himself in the mirror several times. The others dressed in their very best as well. Even Rustic Robin, who is the most caustic regarding "c'vilized people," wore a jacket free of paint stains. I felt rather ashamed of the elaborate ruffles and laces my friends and I wear with hardly a thought, and the young men of our set always fling their hats into any corner. Here are these people so careful with their clothes and so proud of their refinement!

Although I felt proud of our little group as we made our way through the city park, I was a little envious when we passed the large circle of Waxwood belles and beaus, the ladies in the latest fashions, and their scents of rose and lily water filled the air. There was much excitement coming from this group, and I recalled my first months in Waxwood when I had taken part in their laughter. Selma averted her haughty eyes from us, but the others greeted me and some even invited me to join the game. I doubt I should be human if I had not felt a twinge of regret in having to refuse them.

We found a place in the park far away from others, and it was like those evenings in the colony when the breeze is pleasant and people go a-visiting, bringing out their pipes or harmonicas, playing and singing songs. Several artists brought their tools with them and sat sketching people in the park. Some townspeople looked at us with malice, but others were genuinely interested in our work.

I brought my sketchbook too, but I could not find a suitable subject. Perhaps I was at a disadvantage because I knew so many of the people at the picnic. They held no marvel for me, and there was no pose I had not seen before. I noticed Flossie sitting in the grass making a tiny bouquet of dandelions, so I sketched her with her doll, sitting in her lap as she picked the flowers with her careful little fingers. I found myself captivated by the little girl's concentration.

The portrait delighted the girl when I showed it to her. The Potter family is large with three boys and four girls, and I imagine her parents have little patience for this loquacious child.

She pulled me toward the very place I had been avoiding all afternoon where the Potters sat along with the Rosses and several other families who had been hospitable to me last year. The Potters were enchanted by the portrait.

Evan joined me and was most kind to them all, though a little distant. Mr. Alderdice was there too and was most interested in my drawings. I don't mean in an off-hand way, as one would expect from a man so immersed in business. He truly finds art and those who make it fascinating. He thought I captured the magical quality of the child well. I offered to draw him if he would sit for me, in jest, of course. He remarked I ought not to make such an offer, as Evan might not approve. "I have no right to approve or disapprove anything Grace does," Evan answered him.

Mr. Alderdice said, if this were true, then he should have no objection to his asking to see the rest of my drawings. Evan said he had none, but advised me against it. "Mr. Alderdice will only make them wither when he looks upon them with his steely eye." Mr. Alderdice insisted he takes my work as seriously as that of any of his friends. This made Evan livid, as he bowed and said, "The choice is yours, Grace." I knew I would incur Evan's displeasure, but I was curious to hear what Mr. Alderdice would say about my drawings.

He examined each sketch carefully and even found the drawings I had done recently that I neglected to show Evan. I could not resist the allure of my little Tiresias and did several drawings of fish on my own excursions into town alone.

I felt Evan's anger as he glanced at these drawings but he remained silent. Mr. Alderdice asked me why I had chosen such illusive creatures as my subjects. "For the very reason that they are illusive," I answered. Mr. Ross commented on their charm, and Mrs. Ross remarked, "Penelope has an idea about the creatures, Mr. Alderdice." I explained to Mr. Alderdice my theory of the wise little fish and their mythological connection. He agreed there was something all-seeing about them. I was surprise he knew so much about Greek mythology and the blind seer.

He turned to Evan and asked his opinion. Evan answered, "I do not believe in wasting one's talent on frozen subjects." I knew then how disappointed he was that I had gone back to fish after experimenting at the colony. His words wounded me, but, as you and Papa had taught me to keep my wits about me, I said cheerfully that I could see no harm in still-life, and I was as content to draw fish as I was humans or trees.

I was afraid Evan wouldn't speak to me, but when we were with the colony again, he seemed to forget his anger and played games with Verina and all the children. When the others were dozing, took me for a walk around the park. We did not speak much, but this is not unusual. There are many times when there is no need for us to exchange a word.

The fireworks were lovely and the stars added to their sparkle. We were having a pleasant time when Ebba had one of her fits. She plucked some paper and a pencil lying on the grass and pranced over to the belles and beaus sitting near the pier and began to draw under the dim candlelight, her hand moving in twitches and strokes. Selma tried to chase her away with harsh words but to no avail. When Ebba dropped the pencil, a chuckle escaped her throat. She gave Selma the drawing and sauntered off. Selma screamed and flung it down, rushing into the arms of her fiancé. Later, I found the picture sprawled on the grass. Ebba had scribbled a most disturbing portrait of a madwoman, her hair crawling with maggots, her clothing half-torn, and her face riddled with scars. The countenance was unmistakably Selma's.

I returned to the pier where the chatter had died down, and Evan was comforting Ebba. Mr Alderdice stood a little distance away, his hat a little tilted from the wind. He was studying Ebba without disgust or horror, but with a look I shall never be able to describe.

Your loving daughter, Grace

CHAPTER 26

Brandywine, Waxwood, CA July 12, 1853

*D*earest Mama,

It's been unbearably hot here. Waxwood has not experienced such heat in a very long time. I have been feeling unwell since the night of the Fourth. It's nothing that need worry you, only a little dizziness and my appetite is not what it usually is. Ebba is really a wonderful cook, though, and she is a sight to see in the tiny kitchen! She cannot make one soup or one stew. She must make three all at once, and the kitchen looks a muddle by the end of the day. The intensity with which she creates her dishes is sometimes frightening.

Despite my maladies, I have been out now and again. The wax wood forest is sometimes quite shady. I haven't been able to draw much, but I watch others. One would think we were mad, shouting to one another from shack to shack. I don't think one could find the chatter of Bedlam so amusing!

Verina often sits with me. She is such a sweet child, but I don't think she's very artistic, Mama. Her eye for detail and color is rather plain. Ebba wants to believe she has a talent and gave her a small set of paints and a sketchbook for Christmas, but I see how disappointed she is when Verina chooses some other plaything instead. I have interested her in the small checkers set I brought with me from home. Remember how Papa and I used to play after dinner? Verina enjoys the game and, for a six-year-old, she plays very well.

On Saturday, the Pesa Troupe arrived at the colony. They are a theatre group who live similar to us, and every summer, they go about performing operas in parks and city squares for pennies. City theater groups snap up talented performers among them when they come to Lafayette Park, so there is the chance of being discovered besides the money they earn to keep their colony going.

They are a jolly group, these theater folks, and not as immoral as you may think. They brought plenty of elderberry wine with them, which Sivilla and Chadena, two lovely Spanish sisters staying with us, insisted I try because "elderberry is good for the nerves, *angelito*, and when you sick, nerves go bad, eh?" Every morning, they greet the sun with a Spanish dance, and they are beautiful to watch.

Sunday evening was the most joyful occasion, even more so than the Fourth of July. We had a break in the heat as the wind rose from the bay. After the sun had set, we climbed down the hill into the Waxwood city park to watch them perform their opera. The townspeople were kind to them, and Mr. Layton, who owns the largest saloon in town, brought two barrels of beer for the men and cider for the women and children.

When darkness fell, lamps were lit and put in a circle around a wooden platform. We watched the jolly troupe perform Bellini's *Norma*. The opera is fascinating but quite scandalous. If I were to draw Norma, I would make her Lilith. And yet, she has moments of tenderness like her vow of faith to the wretched

Adalgisa when Pollione deceives her. Oh, how men can betray women! Even those who are good and kind like Evan have the power to betray. A moment of capriciousness can snuff out their virtue like a candle flame in the wind.

Dizziness came upon me during the performance. I felt as if bees were stinging my ears and my face. My entire body was aflame, and when I looked down at my hands, they were outlined in red and yellow. I wanted to get away from the loud voices and buzzing bees. Evan was immediately at my side, and I felt his comforting arm around my shoulders. I wanted to tell him to go away because I would burst into flames at any moment and did not want to burn him. I think I shouted at him to stand back. Then everything went black, and the buzzing ceased.

I opened my eyes to find myself in the Rosses' parlor. The windows were open, and the breeze was trickling in. I was no longer aflame and felt quite serene. Beside me sat Mr. Alderdice in a crisp suit and pipe hat. He held out his hands and produced four fresh apricots. "I know how you like them," he said. I ate them slowly, as I was still feeling a little weak, as he watched me with wide, curious eyes. I asked about Evan, and he mumbled something about refreshments in the garden. He had slipped away from the crowd, for he felt responsible for me. We are guardians of one another in Waxwood, for we are both strangers.

After I had eaten the fruit, I tried to sit up, but he insisted I languish on the couch. I asked him to tell me about the last act, as I had missed it because of my fainting spell. He described it with the detail of an astute observer. He then asked me what I thought of the opera. I said it had intrigued me, but was perhaps a little one-sided. "The Madonnas are Madonnas, and the fallen women stay fallen forever. There is no in-between," I pointed out. Mr. Alderdice answered this was as it should be. "For women?" I challenged. "A man may sin and die a sinner just as much as a woman," he objected.

I reminded him Norma had perhaps sinned but her sacrifice

at the end was surely worth redeeming. "One must not judge a woman by a single deed," I said. He asked if I liked the character, and I admitted I felt a bond with her. Mr. Alderdice would not hear of this. "You are more the Casta Diva." The Chaste Goddess? Yes, he would think that. I laugh at it now.

I asked him if he thought Pollione was more virtuous, throwing himself into the pyre to keep the eternal flame burning for the woman he betrayed. He insisted that was redemption, to sacrifice oneself for eternal love. It never would have occurred to me that a man so upright and so business-like could believe in eternal love.

He asked me, rather slyly, if I didn't believe one could sacrifice oneself for a love like Norma and Pollione. After I had returned to the colony, I pondered the question. The books I've read idolize love, but can one really say it exists outside of storybooks? Love rarely bears out in life, as Ebba's own experience shows. I have little experience with love so far, but, although I am not as embittered as she, I am uncertain.

Your loving daughter, Grace

CHAPTER 27

Brandywine, Waxwood, CA July 15, 1853

*D*earest Mama,

Forgive my unsteady hand. You ought to understand me, even if my writing is shaky. You have always understood me.

I am ill again. It's nothing serious, but quite odd. I never had to carry smelling salts about with me like other young ladies on Rincon Hill, and my appetite has always been hearty. Now I must have smelling salts with me, and though my appetite is more voracious than before, I sometimes cannot keep it down.

I am sure it is the heat. It must be the heat!

The coolness under the wax wood trees has ceased, and the other day when I touched one, my hand left an imprint. I coaxed Evan to carve our initials in it, but he looked at me as if I were mad. Perhaps it was childish of me.

Oh, it's hot as coals here! These little shacks, so lovely, I used to think. But now — well, I remember hearing about the tribes and their clay ovens when I was a child, flames bursting out of the red stone pits. My room at the Jones' is like that. I swear I can see red spots around me in the afternoon heat. The flames, oh, the flames!

I no longer go to the woods (what is the point if there is no shelter from the heat?) I can't sit outside for long. Though it's better than the clay oven, I cannot stand to see poor little Verina with her hair flying about and her dress sticking to her legs and arms. And yet, she smiles all the time. I suppose children can endure anything.

Evan has been talking of leaving Brandywine and finding work as an architecture in the city. He hints he might persuade Mr. Sprout, the man who introduced him to the colony, to give him a position as a drafter. He frightens me with his talk. I know he would rather die than leave Brandywine. His soul would die, anyway.

Mr. Alderdice assures me he will not do it. I speak with him frequently now because I visit the Rosses when I can. I have not fainted again, but fear of it brings me down the hill where the heat is not so bold. This boiling summer in Waxwood has been all over the papers. You really ought to read the papers, Mama, though I know how much you dislike their Grim Reaper words. We must know what is happening around us, mustn't we? We cannot stay pent up in our luxurious lair. We must know the evil men do or some such thing. Evil does not disappear when we shut our eyes.

What morbid words I write! Do not worry, Mama. There is no evil here. Waxwood is as pure as the white gates of heaven. My spirits rise when I am at the Rosses'. It is so much cooler there. I like to sit in the parlor with the windows open. The bay brings in such a lovely breeze. Why can't it rise just a little further up the hill?

Mr. Alderdice can be quite amusing. He is like a mother hen to me. Bertha, dear old-fashioned Bertha, always tries to pull him out with the belles and beaus, but he is disinterested. He gives her that austere smile and makes excuses. I scolded him for it, as a simple "no" would be much more honest, and he is always talking about honesty, is he not? He answers me, "Though she is a silly goose, she deserves politeness."

The other day he told me a little about himself. His father had been more out of work than in it, and the squalor of their life in Flesa wore down his mother. His brothers constantly cried for bread, so he came to San Francisco to find work at the age of fourteen. His constant toil taught him to despise those who "fiddle with life." It is true in our set the young men waste their hours at the Hercules Club and the young ladies at the milliners. Their most serious contemplations take place in the ballrooms, deciding with whom they will and will not dance!

I wonder if he thinks I am a fiddler with life too. I feel certain he did at one time, but not now. He speaks to me about so many meaningful subjects my mind cannot recall them. He reiterates often his vow that he is my friend and will help me if I should ever need it. I cannot think what he means.

When I take my leave, he invites me to return to the house, to my old room with the pleasant peach curtains and sweet scent of roses. It is not his house, yet he invites me as if it is. But that is his way, isn't it?

Your loving daughter, Grace

CHAPTER 28

Waxwood, CA July 26, 1853

*D*earest Mama,
　　I am back at the Rosses' in my old room. My health improves every day. I told you, Mama, there was no need for you to be concerned. The heat still looms, but not as ferociously as it did before. I don't want to go back to Brandywine. I've had my little adventure for the summer. Isolation does not make a place safer when one is a stranger in a strange world. Strangeness is comforting until it is no longer strange. If I speak in circles, forgive me, for I am still a little dazed at times.

　　Mr. Alderdice and I talk about the city quite often. We share a common affection for San Francisco. We reminisce about walks in Lafayette Park and the opera and watching the passengers disembark steamships on the wharf. San Francisco's familiarity comforts me. I did not feel this way a year ago. I loved it no less, but it had become full of demons. But one can still love the demons of one's strange shadows.

I am drawing again, and I rather think my fish are looking almost human. I feel like Titania getting back to life after having been asleep for a long time. One must move forward, always move forward, Mama. I am not ready to give up the life here, but I am making the strange familiar to me again. One must move on.

Mr. Alderdice accompanies me to visits with the belles and beaus, who have all welcomed me back. We watch them splashing about in their rowboats or playing croquet. (Do you know I love the game more than I did in the city?) Sometimes our mood is thoughtful, and we speak of serious subjects. Other times, we are capricious and whisper together about the little intrigues we observe like two gossips. Mr. Alderdice's direct way of putting things no longer irks me. I admit to being callous at times, but he is always respectful. I view their coquetry with disgust, and the men are just as bad as the women. And yet, how else is one to marry? I must marry. There is no other way. I must marry *somebody*.

Evan is unhappy I returned to the Rosses. He came often when I was ill, but Mr. Alderdice proved a diligent watcher and forbade him to see me. I was too weak to resist. I know Evan has been going down to the pier, enticing summer visitors to sit for portraits with his charm and lightheartedness. Summer is when the Brandywine artists earn the most from their work, as tourists have been discovering what a pleasant place Waxwood is. Mr. Ross predicts the town shall one day become like those resort spots popping up in the East. He is not looking forward to it.

I miss Evan, Ebba, Verina and all the people at the colony. Sweet memories tug at my heart of mornings among the wax trees and blackberry bushes, evenings in the garden waiting to see who will visit and where their conversations will take us. Lately I prefer to listen more than take part. I once had high expectations of myself, but it's almost a relief to let them go. I'm sure it must be my poor health.

This morning, Mr. Alderdice did not join me in my morning walk, and when I reached the pier, Evan was lingering near the rocks. He ran forth and took my hands, holding his cheek to mine. A few fishermen grinned and politely moved to the other side of the pier.

I was elated to see him, of course. He lavished adorations upon me and begged me to come back to Brandywine. I told him as tenderly as I could that the heat still affected me, and I might come back when the summer was over, if I did not return to San Francisco.

He was annoyed and said, "I'm sure Mr. Alderdice is looking after you very well." I reminded him Mr. Alderdice is Papa's clerk, and it's only natural he should be concerned for me. "You weren't so partial toward him when you spoke of him last year," he reminded me. This is true, Mama, but I know Mr. Alderdice better now, and while he is still a little too precise for my taste, his company is not unpleasant. I said as much to Evan. He accused me of preferring "fawning fools" over friends who understood and encourage my artistic endeavors. I turned away, as I did not want him to see my tears. When I turned back again, he was gone.

But it is not Evan's way to remain angry for long. While we were at dinner, Tillie slipped me a card. It contained a pencil drawing of myself and Evan in the wax wood forest walking hand in hand, and so tender did we look that it brought tears to my eyes. He had scrawled,

"WHILE I AM I, and you are you,
   So long as the world contains us both,
   Me the loving and you the loth,
   While the one eludes, must the other pursue."
   Forgive me.

. . .

I HAVE FORGIVEN HIM. He is so sincere and loving, I shall make good on my promise to return to him when this terrible heat subsides.

Your loving daughter, Grace

CHAPTER 29

Waxwood, CA August 3, 1853

$\mathcal{D}$earest Mama,
    I was ashamed of my behavior toward Evan. I felt wonderful today, so I took the ferry to Brandywine. The artists welcomed me with open arms. Ebba held me close for a long time, and Verina treated me as if I were a long-lost aunt. Their graciousness warmed me, though I cannot think what I did to deserve it.

Evan took me to our favorite place in the wax woods, and there, among the blackberry bushes and the wild flowers, he proposed marriage. It was all quite romantic and unconventional. He offered me a ring, a lovely thing with a sapphire cradled in diamonds that had been his grandmother's. He promised he would speak to Papa, and if Papa didn't approve of his life at Brandywine, he would leave Ebba and Verina in the little house with the red roof and return to the architectural firm in San Francisco, if they will have him. If not, he will find work elsewhere. He is profoundly sincere about providing for me in any way Papa wishes, even if it means leaving the artistic life he loves to make his fortune in the city.

I am as pleased as any young lady who receives her first proposal, but do not think for a moment, Mama, that I would act in haste. I asked him to give me time to consider, as I know Papa will want to know more about him. Evan said he would wait six months or a year if I should wish it.

I told Mr. Alderdice because I didn't forget his vow of friendship to me, and one needs a gentleman friend at such a time. We took an afternoon walk, as the sun had taken refuge in the clouds. As you may imagine, he had definite opinions on the matter. He assured me he has no intention of interfering, but thinks I would be making a grave mistake if I married Evan.

I asked if this was because Evan is not wealthy or of Society. He replied it was neither of those, as no one knew better than himself there is more than one way for a man to get on in the world. "Mr. Jones is not what he appears to be," he said. He took hold of my arm and promised he would refrain from telling me of Evan's past evils, as I might turn against him rather than Evan, which I thought was quite calculating.

"You hate Evan enough to want him out of my life?" I asked. He paused for what seemed like a long time before he answered, "I love you enough to want you to marry me instead."

I've known for some time that Mr. Alderdice had intentions toward me. I realized it in the way he watched me when he came to the house for tea, and in the way his eyes followed me when I came to Papa's office. I told him I honored his sentiments but I could never consider him as more than a friend. Mr. Alderdice said, "And if I were to tell you that your acquaintance with Mr. Jones did not come about by chance?" That rather flustered me. He went on, "he bargains for his own gain, you see." I'm sure he meant to insinuate Evan was marrying me because I will one day be an heiress to one of the largest shipping companies in San Francisco.

He was quite melancholy when we returned to the Rosses. He hardly ate any dinner, and later when we sat in the parlor, he chewed the end of his pipe, staring at the empty fireplace. When I rose to go to bed, he followed me and asked if I had definitely decided to marry Evan. I told him I didn't know yet, which is quite true. He repeated his accusation that Evan was not who he seemed. I again asked him to explain, but he evaded my questions, saying, "Let us say he is not worthy of you." He reiterated what he has always told me: He is my friend, and I should not hesitate to apply to him for help if I need it.

Mr. Alderdice has always been honest with me, but he has designs. I'm sure of that. I won't decide about the proposal until I return to San Francisco, but be sure of one thing, Mama. I mean to marry. I *must* marry.

Your loving daughter, Grace

CHAPTER 30

Waxwood, CA August 6, 1853

*D*earest Mama,

There is a summer storm raging outside my window. The noise of the bay as it swells up in the sky is like the cry of whales. Do you remember when Papa took us to see the whales when I was a child? They are formidable creatures, to be sure, but oh, their cries broke my heart!

The party is still going in the garden. I can hear a flute dancing among the solemn strings. They are playing "Casta Diva." I am sure Mr. Alderdice asked them to play it, hoping to lure me back into the garden. I think he has some idea I favored this opera because I told him I felt an affinity with Norma. Or perhaps it was Evan who asked them to play it. I am no longer sure where one ends and the other begins. Where one loves, the other takes up the thread of love...

But I won't go back down, though I know how much joy it

brings Bertha, dear, old-fashioned Bertha, to see her devoted friends gather round her on her twentieth birthday.

Bertha toiled the entire week about the theme for her party. She asked me to draw her ideas on paper, but nothing pleased her. She finally agreed to her mother's suggestion of a Japanese theme, and the delicate atmosphere suits Bertha exactly. We worried the wind would tear into the paper lanterns, but they survived, glowing with lovely streaks of lights all over the garden. Evan came early and helped us pin sheets of silk of peach and pale pink for the pavilion. Against the black night, the effects was magical.

Ebba did not come. Evan confessed she has been roaming the forest alone at night in her artist's frock stained with clay, and sometimes he finds her asleep under a tree in the morning. He does his best to hide it from Verina. But that child with her inquisitive eyes — oh, how she alarmed me sometimes! Worse than my fish.

I drew Bertha a mermaid as a birthday gift. I set out to draw a butterfly of a girl with flowing hair and naïve eyes like Bertha's. But my awkward hand turned her into a rather knobby thing with tangled hair and narrow eyes. Mr. Alderdice said she looked more like a petulant child than a mermaid, but I find her countenance more sinister. She gazes at one with one false eye and one caustic, daring anyone to stare back at her. The picture did not turn out as I imagined it, but does anything in life?

Of course Bertha forgave me. She has forgiven me so much for so long. But some things are unforgivable. I'm sure if Bertha knew some things about me, she would cease to forgive me. Good, kind, Bertha. Looking at her now makes me shudder.

Am I talking nonsense, Mama? It has been a confusing evening. The chaos of the party, the paper lanterns with their lights shining in my eyes, the dancing. And now the orchestra playing "Casta Diva". It is too much!

I cannot go down again tonight, no, no! The dizziness has

come back. I feel almost like one of those lanterns, swinging in the wind, afraid it will fly me away. I stood it as long as I could for Bertha's sake. But, lost in the crowd, I felt suddenly as if I wanted to get away. Someone pushed a champagne glass into my hands. I threw it in the grass and escaped to the front porch.

The wind turned into a caressing breeze. I closed my eyes and let its airy hand brush my face. Do you remember you used to caress my cheek before I went to bed when I was a child? You said it would make me sleep better, and you were right. A little girl needs her mother's caresses, but a big girl must go without them. I should not want to caress my little girl or little boy's cheek so she or he will endure the pain of having it withdrawn when they are older. Little girl, little boy — oh, which?

I heard a clatter of heels, and I thought some of the belles escaped their beaus and had come out to get some fresh air. I walked toward the other side of the veranda so they wouldn't see me. But the crashing feet did not belong to giggling young ladies. I recognized Evan's booming voice and, alongside it, Mr. Alderdice's more reserved tone.

The latter was saying he had no interest in Evan's undying love for me. He wished to see Evan later that night. He wished to make Evan a proposition.

The wind suddenly turned to ice and I crush my handkerchief to my face. I could only imagine Mr. Alderdice's "proposition" had something to do with the marriage proposal. I know it has been on Mr. Alderdice's mind. We never spoke of it again, but he watches me with disarming eyes as if he were trying to pierce my thoughts.

Evan insisted he had no wish to hear of any proposition he might have to offer. Mr. Alderdice answered that it would be in my best interest as well as his own if he were not so ornery. Words crossed in the wind so I did not hear the reply. I wanted to rush upstairs and shut myself up in may room, but my feet would not move.

I don't know what Mr. Alderdice said in that moment, but whatever it was, Evan agreed to allow him to come to the colony after the party, though he smirked of how the man of finance may find the place uncomfortable. Mr. Alderdice suggested somewhere private, the wax wood forest perhaps, but Evan refused. "I cannot leave my sister alone so late at night."

"No," Mr. Alderdice answered. "I'm sure you can't."

Silence followed, and I thought they had both returned to the party. Then, Even said he knew what Mr. Alderdice thought of him and perhaps he had not behaved toward me in the most honorable manner in the past, but he would do right by me now. He intended to leave Brandywine and return to San Francisco. "She will never have cause to regret marrying me," he promised. I was deeply touched to hear him telling this to a man he scarcely admired but realized meant something to my father and to me.

Mr. Alderdice answered he could well imagine what sort of life Evan would give me. "A dirty little flat downtown, reeking of onions, children screaming loud enough for the entire neighborhood to hear, and a society of charlatans masquerading as 'artists' whose morals would turn a fine woman like Penelope into a—" He stopped, too sickened to go on.

Evan insisted he would do right by me. "You have already done wrong by her," Mr. Alderdice thundered. "You have already done the unforgivable."

The same blackness that closed in on me the day of the opera threatened to do so now, so I scurried to my room where I locked the door and I shall not open it for anyone. A part of me wants to know, must know. But I am like one of Ebba's clay sculptures, leaden and useless. Oh, how a woman does wrong when she has been taught not to follow her instincts!

Your loving daughter, Grace

CHAPTER 31

Waxwood, CA August 9, 1853

*D*earest Mama,
This morning I discovered a bird's nest in the tree behind the house. Their gibbering awakened me out of the first deep sleep I've had since Bertha's party. Four little birds caw, their mouths open, waiting for their mother to come back with food. Not since I was a little girl has the miracle of life intrigued me. How many little creatures did I bring back from Prathe Woods despite Papa scolding, "It's cruel to separate the babe from the mother." I only wanted to look at them. It still elates me to see something new begin from something that has ended.

Evan has withdrawn his proposal. I feel as if my world has come crashing down around me. I had decided to marry him, though I wouldn't have told him so until you and Papa had consented. I don't know what pains me more — his withdrawal or his false reasoning. He insists he cannot marry me because he will never have anything to give me. But he has given me my art and his love, and that is everything!

When I told him this, he murmured, "It is not enough." I thought he meant the colony, and I assured him I would gladly live the humble life of the artists. He insisted I deserved more, and am destined for more. "Mr. Alderdice can give you what you deserve, Grace," he admitted. "His prospects are bright, and he is ambitious." I was honest with him and told him Mr. Alderdice and I are friends, but I do not love him. "There are other things to think of besides love," he said. "You must think of them, Grace. You must think of them now." Yes, there are other things to think of besides love. I am not so naïve as to believe love may conquer all.

He insisted it would be best if we did not see one another again. My heart sank at the thought of never hearing him speak of art or recite poetry again. Those petty pleasures seem absurd to me now. He said, "I advise you to marry Malcolm and return to the city where you belong."

I am too saddened right now to think. I should like to go home. Yes, I should like to go home.

Your loving daughter, Grace

CHAPTER 32

Waxwood, CA August 14, 1853

$\mathscr{D}$earest Mama,
        I accepted Malcolm's proposal. We take the stage-coach back to the city tomorrow and, if you and Papa agree, we will marry in a few weeks. I will be glad to see you and Papa and all our friends again!

It has been a long and arduous year. I am resigned to my fate. It is not altogether filled with misery and unhappiness. I have my health back and my wits about me, and I mean to hold on to both.

Today was fish market day, and I couldn't resist one last trek to the pier. Malcolm teased me about being less whimsical when we return to the city. He is right, of course. When one is to begin one's course in life, one must be steady, come what may. Life holds many surprises, doesn't it?

We convinced Bertha and the Rosses to come with us. Poor

dear Bertha, she has done little but weep since I announced I was going to marry Malcolm and return to San Francisco. I don't know which upsets her more. She hangs on me as if she is trying to absorb my company as much as possible before I leave. Malcolm has as little patience with babbling, weeping fools as he has the life-fiddling fools. But he is, as always, courteous to her.

The market was crowded with people and birds. Malcolm was trying to amuse me by playing with a crab when suddenly we heard a scream. A little boy was crying and pointing to the ground. A gull was attacking one of the fish lying on the table. No one would go near it except for Malcolm and I. By the time we chased it away, the gull had eaten the eyes and part of the belly.

I would have fainted had Malcolm not led me away and procured a libation which returned my spirits. As we walked home, I was haunted by the memory of my meeting with Evan the year before. Some people leave their imprint on our souls even when they abandon us.

I realize now life's expectations of us is as vital as our expectations of life. For better or worse, life's expectations hang around our necks like a stone necklace. Do you remember we once saw a sapphire necklace in an obscure little shop in Chinatown? They say sapphires represent purity and protects against treachery. I went back to that little shop to try it on, but the moment I put it around my throat, I felt smothered by its weight. Life's expectations are like that sapphire necklace, but one must drag it around one's neck just the same.

I am sorry to sound so grave, Mama. I know I shall be more cheerful once I reach the city.

I know you save all my letters, but I don't want Papa or Malcolm to ever find those I wrote you from Waxwood. So please send them to Evan. I would like him to have them so he may know I am not angry with him.

Your loving daughter, Penelope

P.S. - I AM BACK to calling myself Penelope. Malcolm prefers it. — PC

CHAPTER 33

*B*y the time the morning sunshine spread a canopy of light over her bed, Vivian had put the last letter down, her eyes open and alert. How silent it was here without the noise of horses and horns awakening the city and maids scurrying about in their rustling skirts. She wonder ed whether her grandmother had also felt this her first weeks at Brandywine with no expectations weighing her down like a sapphire necklace.

Vivian had only seen it once when she was a child. She had been watching her grandmother dress for a ball, and Grandfather strolled in, fingered the jewelry box on the vanity, and pulled out the necklace. Clear blue stones flashed in the rose-shaped center. She had never seen her grandfather handle anything delicately, but he laid it on the table in front of Grandmother.

Mrs. Cross, Grandmother's lady's maid, who lived up to her name, was, for once, in awe. "Why do you never wear it, ma'am?"

Grandmother fingered the rose with tears in her eyes. She put it back in the jewelry box and wore her diamond broach that night instead.

Vivian understood now why the specter from Grandmother's debutante portrait followed her like a figure in the mist since she arrived in Waxwood. She understood why there would be no peace unless she continued to twist the dagger until the phantom was dead.

Verina opened it halfway but did not enter. "Breakfast will be ready in a few minutes. You mustn't leave without food." The last word faded as she stared at the pile of letters on the bed.

As Vivian adjusted the combs in her hair, the sharp needles dug into her fingers. So Verina *had* read the letters. Or Evan had read them to her, or she had read them to Evan. She had lied about knowing nothing, and Vivian suspected even without reading the letters, her memory was not as poor as she claimed. *Children see and hear. They see and hear everything!*

Verina had set out brown bread and cheese, coffee, and a bowl of blackberries. They looked like the dregs of a banquet that had ended a long time ago.

Seeing her eyes on fixed on the blackberries, Verina smiled. "There's a patch near here."

"I know," Vivian said. The woman's hand shook a little as she poured her a cup of coffee. "You haven't been completely honest with me, have you?"

Verina stared into her empty plate.

"I noticed the look on your face when you saw the letters," Vivian continued.

"I read them after Uncle Evan died," she admitted. "I had a right. She left them to him and he left what little he had to me."

"He must have read them."

"He read them, yes," she said. "Over and over and over again." She looked at Vivian with cold eyes.

"And did your mother read them after he died?" Vivian asked.

"My mother went into an asylum five months after Grace left." The tone held no emotion.

Vivian reached to cover her hand. "I'm sorry."

"You needn't be," she said. "She had the best care at the Glock-pool Sanatorium. Uncle Evan saw to it."

"I'm glad," said Vivian.

The woman gave her a fierce look. "Now that you've read the letters, you see there is nothing more I can tell you."

"I think there is much more you can tell me."

"I've told you all I know."

Vivian took her hand. "Verina, I wish I could make you see our specters intertwine, and we could help one another be free of them."

The woman snatched her hand away. "I don't go chasing after phantoms."

"They come chasing after you," Vivian said.

The woman heaved a sob and buried her face in her hands. Vivian remained silent, letting her weep. "You loved your uncle very much, didn't you?" She asked softly.

"He was a sweet, thoughtful man who always tried to do right by everyone."

"And you liked my grandmother in spite of what happened, didn't you?"

The woman's features went from stone to wax. "Yes. I liked her. Until Uncle Evan took sick. She haunted him until the day he died."

"Haunted?" Vivian stared at her.

"He once said sometimes doing right can eat away one's life."

Vivian wandered to the window and parted the curtains. The sun's harsh heat burned her skin. "Perhaps his own guilt haunted him, not my grandmother."

Verina's face was white like marble as she poured Vivian another cup of coffee. "He had nothing to feel guilty about," she said. "He did what he did for *her*."

"And it was the tragedy of his life," Vivian guessed.

"It was obviously not the tragedy of hers," she snapped. "Your grandmother had no qualms about marrying Malcolm Alderdice nor living in a big house and fancying herself the belle of San Francisco society."

"She had little choice," Vivian retorted. "He withdrew his proposal of marriage."

"He wouldn't have if she had come back to Brandywine when he asked her to!" Verina's voice grew shrill. "She chose to stay with her friends and Malcolm Alderdice."

"It was he who no longer wished to marry her," Vivian mumbled.

"Because he knew he could never give her what she wanted," the woman insisted. "He sacrificed his own happiness for her avarice!"

Vivian strolled into her room and returned with the letters. She held them out to Verina. The woman winced. "I don't want to read them again!"

"Read only the summer letters."

"What for?"

"Help me solve the riddle," she pleaded.

"There is no riddle!" Verina insisted. "My uncle let Grace go so she could marry your grandfather and live in San Francisco society."

Vivian placed the letters from the summer of 1853 in front of her. "Please."

As the woman read, Vivian stared out the window. The garden looked like a faded photograph compared to the way her grandmother had described it. The grass was a drab yellow, and the flowers drooped as if they were wary. There was no sign of life in any of the other houses.

Verina flung the letters away. "Only words!"

"Not when one reads between the lines." Vivian started counting fingers, but then stopped herself.

The woman rose. "It's as I told you, Vivian."

Vivian slid into a chair. "It was all strange and sudden, wasn't it?"

Verina sighed. "That hardly matters."

She watched the woman collect the plates, the cups and

saucers. Her hands plucked at the delicate china. "You don't believe a web of lies hides between those lines?"

Verina dropped a saucer on the floor. She did not pick it up. "Why do you say such things?"

"None of it makes sense," Vivian insisted. "The proposal. The conversation between your uncle and my grandmother at the birthday party. Your Uncle Evan withdraws his proposal for reasons even my grandmother didn't believe." She took the woman's arm. "Did my grandfather come to the colony that night?"

Verina looked down at her wet hands. "Yes."

"What did they talk about?"

The woman did not answer.

"You must have understood something, even as a child," Vivian said. "Grandmother said you were inquisitive. You must know *something*."

"I didn't want to know!" Verina backed away.

Vivian clutched her black handkerchief. "Perhaps I would judge her harshly too, if I didn't know what she went back to and how she suffered for it as much as your uncle."

"What right do you have to come here with your phantoms and try to make them mine?" Verina's shriek echoed the piercing call of a bird. "My uncle was a good man. Better than your Malcolm Alderdice!"

"Perhaps he was," Vivian murmured.

"He took care of Mama," she continued. "He made sure she didn't end up like his mother in a state asylum."

"That must have cost a great deal."

"It cost him Grace!" Verina glared at her. "He kept me from going mad too. He was so strong, so clear about everything." The woman looked at her with demon eyes. "Go home and leave your specter in the shadows where she belongs."

"I couldn't live with that the rest of my life." She held the handkerchief to her lips.

Verina turned back to the dishes. "I can no longer help you. If you insist on following this specter of yours, find someone else to help you."

Vivian looked at her. "And who will help you, Verina?" The woman's hands grasped the dishes she had set on the table. "Your mother wanted you to leave Brandywine." She put her hands on the woman's shoulders. "I offered to help you yesterday and I meant it."

"I'll stay here," said Verina. "Just as Uncle Evan would have wanted."

"Your mother wanted—"

"My loyalty is to him, not her!"

Vivian left the kitchen, and the woman did not follow her. She fit the hat and veil over her head, then picked up her reticule, placing the letters inside. She put all the money she had on the table, knowing it would be paltry comfort to a woman who insisted on living with a shadow.

As she walked back to town, she thought of what Verina had said: *Find someone else to help you.* Only one person could help her now, the one person who held the family Unmentionables in the palm of her hand.

~~~~~

Vivian could not leave Waxwood without returning to the criss-cross house on Mueller Street. The blue shutters were closed, but Vivian found Ruth sitting on the veranda gazing into the naked grass. She jumped when she saw Vivian. "You're still here!"

"I stayed the night with Verina," she said.

"Mama was disappointed you didn't come back," came the caustic reply. "She found the drawing."

Vivian was silent for a moment. "I'd like to tell your mother goodbye." She hesitated. "And to thank her. If she hadn't come to the funeral, I might never have known anything about my grandmother's past life."

"Perhaps it would have been better if you hadn't." There was a smirk on Ruth's face. "Have you chased it down now, this specter of yours?"

"Not entirely," said Vivian.

"I thought Verina could help you."

Vivian looked down at the rough wood. "What she wouldn't say helped me more than what she would."

"Evan was all she had," said Ruth. "Her mother was placed in an asylum when she was very young."

"I wish there was more I could do for her." Vivian thought of the money she left on the table. "May I see your mother now?"

"She's asleep." The woman said "Mama sleeps restlessly ever since her legs gave way. I'm loath to wake her."

"Don't, then," said Vivian. "I would like to see the picture, if I may."

Ruth disappeared through the back door and returned with the mermaid. Her eyes filled with tears as she made out the imprint of the mermaid.

"Is it what you expected?" The woman asked.

Vivian thought back to the letter: *The picture did not turn out as I imagined it, but does anything in life?* "One mustn't put too much faith in expectations."

"I don't think my mother likes it much," Ruth admitted. "One cannot deny it has *something*."

"Yes," Vivian said. "Something." She sighed. "Thank you for showing it to me."

"You may keep it if you like," the woman said.

Vivian dabbed her eyes. "It belongs here where my grand-mother was free."

Ruth cocked her head. "Just what *did* you find out, if I may ask?"

Vivian considered telling her about the letters, but she recalled Verina's fear and her rejection. "I found out why Penelope was called Grace." Ruth stared at her. "Evan gave her the name. He thought it suited her better."

"What an odd reason!"

Vivian smiled a little. "You might tell your mother. She was curious."

Ruth nodded.

Vivian hesitated. "It might also reassure her to know Grace went back to Penelope when she returned to San Francisco."

"Why did she go back?"

Vivian turned around. "To the name?"

"The name," said Ruth. "And the place. Her old life."

Vivian's thoughts were moving as swiftly as the early morning wind. "It was like the sapphire necklace. She couldn't escape it."

Ruth chuckled. "You really are vague sometimes, Vivian."

"Talking in circles, my mother calls it." She smiled. "But even with circles, one ends a little wiser than one began."

When she reached the street, she turned and saw Ruth standing on the front steps. She waved. The woman's face remained grave, but she returned the goodbye.

CHAPTER 34

The train pulled into the San Francisco station just as the fog lifted off the bay. Through rods of steam, the water looked dismal and alienating. Vivian wondered why there was no fish market in San Francisco on Sundays.

She waved away the porter's offer to hail a hackney. The air was tense and chilly, and people glanced at her veiled face as if she had no business being there. She saw Mrs. Lang, a neighbor of theirs, fiddling with her bag as a porter waited to help her on the train. The woman's face slacked when she saw Vivian, making Vivian aware of her quick walk. She ignored the woman's greeting and crossed Stockton and into Chinatown. Her mother always avoided the neighborhood, but Vivian and Jake had once ventured into the narrow lanes, admiring the vibrant colors and ornaments thrown on tables outside for all to see. She blended with throngs of people whose stares were more curious than condemning. She lifted her veil, her curiosity equal to those around her.

A jewelry store stretched into the triangular corner of Washington and Stockton. Green, white, and blue stones flashed in her eyes. A tiny woman with a smooth face peered out. "You like? You want to see?" Vivian tried to lower her veil, but the wind blew it back. The woman glanced at the sun. "Plenty hot, plenty hot. You come inside." She took Vivian's hand, her touch cool and soothing.

The shop was larger than it looked through the window. The woman's eyes were keen as her smile softened. "You like?" She pointed to the display in the window. Vivian stared at the sapphire necklace. "You try, you see." Icy pearls clasped around Vivian's throat. The woman scurried behind a beaded curtain and came out with a hand mirror. The sapphire shone vivid blue inside a cradle of diamonds. The sun hit the sapphire, showing its transparent blue as sharp as her grandfather's eyes.

She lamented, "An elegant hangman's noose."

"Beg pardon?" the woman asked.

Vivian heard the voice of another in her own. That other was the debutante in the pink dress and pink pearls. That other had escaped he confinement to Waxwood, filled her lungs with the breath of freedom, and then gone back into her cage like a chained circus animal that ran away and, when caught, dutifully pranced back into its prison. That other was her specter, sending her a warning. But where could Vivian escape? She had no Waxwood, no Brandywine, and no Evan.

The air became still, the two sides of the triangular room closing in. She backed away, trying to deepen the space, and hit the corner between the two windows spilling into two cross streets. *Life's expectations are like that sapphire necklace, but one must drag it around one's neck just the same.*

She gave a cry and, tearing off the necklace, ran out of the shop.

~~~~~

By the time Vivian reached Alderdice Hall, her nerves had settled. She lingered inside the hall for a moment, her hand at her throat. She felt the sapphire still around her neck, pulling her down, determined to entomb her.

A cough echoed in the hollow entrance, and Basset stood with his usual unruffled countenance. "The family is at breakfast, miss."

She never liked Basset's ceremonial ways, but she was grateful to him at that moment for bringing her back to the present. Her hand dropped from her throat.

Larissa sat in her usual chair with another bundle of condolence letters beside her half-finished plate. Jake's figure pointed toward the chandelier, signaling he had just received a verbal beating. Grandfather's breakfast lay untouched in front of him. The familiar scene reminded Vivian of when Bertha Ross' letter had arrived only two days before.

"Here she is, Father," Larissa sang out. "Didn't I tell you Vivian was due to arrive at any moment, and you needn't worry?" Her mother gave her a fierce smile. "I really ought to be furious with you, dear."

Vivian could tell her mother was, in fact, furious. Despite the light tone, the angular features carved through her pale skin, and her forehead wrinkled with agitation. "Mother, I must talk to you." Her voice sounded rough and dim.

"How are the Hogans?" Larissa gave Vivian a warning look. Vivian understood she had told Grandfather some lie about her having been with the Hogans.

"We must talk, Mother," she repeated. "In private."

The well-balanced lightness disappeared from her mother's face. "Later, dear."

"Yes, what?" Grandfather shouted as if he had just awakened from a dream.

"I told you Vivian stayed with the Hogans last night, Father," Larissa said.

"Viv had to get away from the morbid atmosphere here, Grandfather." Jake played along.

She looked from her mother to her brother, feeling the silent conspiracy between them. "Yes, I've been with the Hogans, Grandfather."

The old man looked at her with faded eyes. "Didn't like death either, she didn't."

"No," Vivian said softly. "I don't believe she did."

Lines appeared at the corners of Larissa's mouth. "Go upstairs and change, Vivian." she said in a low voice.

"I'll change once we've talked."

"I'm not asking you, Vivian." The tone was knife-sharp.

"I didn't imagine you were," she sighed.

"Same dress, same dress!" Grandfather's eye flew open and he regarded her with a tart look.

"Your grandfather doesn't like to see you in the same dress," Larissa said. "You've already tormented him this morning."

"Have I?" Vivian stared down at the spotless tablecloth.

"He was anxious about you." Her mother lowered her voice. "We found him in your room this morning."

Vivian examined the man sitting at the end of the table. The morning paper lay in the rack next to him, untouched like his eggs and toast. His fingers curled around the coffee cup, but he did not drink. His eyes blinked at Vivian, and she wondered whom he was really seeing.

"It's time Grandfather ate his meals in his room," Vivian said.

"Vivian." Larissa's voice sounded defeated.

She touched her mother's hand. "Mother, we must stop these games."

Jake pushed his chair back and wandered out.

"Now you've upset your brother," said Larissa in a sharp voice.

"I shouldn't think that would disturb you much, Mother." Vivian felt bolder now. "Just as Grandmother's death didn't seem to disturb you much."

A spoon dropped on the floor. Larissa did not bend down to

pick it up. "I asked you to go upstairs and change. I won't ask again."

Vivian looked at her for a moment, then stepped out into the hall.

"And then come down again," Larissa called.

"I wish to be alone for a while."

"Your wishes, dear," Larissa said in a haughty tone, "are of no importance at the moment."

"Duty calls, my dear, duty calls," Grandfather said brightly, then lapsed back into bewilderment.

"I have done my duty, Grandfather," Vivian said. "More than you will ever know."

"I shall expect you in the downstairs parlor after you've changed," said her mother.

"I'll do everything you wish," Vivian said, "if you do the one thing for me." Larissa gave her an inquisitive look. "You agree to have a private conversation with me."

"About the promise you broke?" At last, her mother had said it.

"Yes, in a manner of speaking," said Vivian.

"You know I don't like quarrels."

"This won't be a quarrel, Mother," she said. "It shall be a clarification."

Larissa closed her eyes. "Pull the cord for Basset, dear. Your grandfather has finished his breakfast."

Vivian gave her a steady look. "Will you agree, Mother?"

Larissa glared.

"For once!" Tears wet Vivian's cheeks. "For once."

A corner of Larissa's mouth softened, recognizing her daughter's distress. "Of course, dear."

As Vivian started up the stairs, she heard Larissa tell Basset that Grandfather would take his meals in his room from now on.

CHAPTER 35

*V*ivian spent most of the day rereading the letters until the ink was smudged. When the hall clock struck nine, she slipped a wrap over her nightgown and made her way to Larissa's room, the letters in hand.

Her mother was in bed, working on her embroidery. She caught Vivian's eye, then placed the needlework aside. "This is a surprise, dear."

"You promised you would speak to me privately," Vivian reminded her.

"It's terribly late." Larissa sighed. "Reverend Norris told me you may see him whenever you wish, you know."

"I don't want to talk about grandmother's death." Vivian held the letters close to her chest. "I want to talk about her life."

"Please, Vivian." Larissa sighed. "Not tonight."

"I only want you read some letters." Vivian tried to control her anger. "It won't take long."

"I'm too tired to read anything."

Glass prisms near the window shook from the wind, giving out a voluptuous ring. Jake had once said the truth could howl like church bells. She put the letters on the blanket. "She wrote Great-Grandmother from Waxwood."

"I see." Larissa's tone was soft.

"She was there a long time. Much longer than a summer."

"This was why I wanted you to never speak of it again," said her mother. "I knew it would disturb you."

"Disturb?" The word made Vivian laugh. "I'm no longer disturbed, Mother. I expected half-truths from you, and I got them."

Larissa opened her mouth to reprimand, but something stopped her. The wind chimes kept time with her mother's sliding fingers as she went through the letters. The bells let out a mocking ring. Vivian leapt up and shut the window.

When her mother put the letter down, she looked neither surprised nor horrified. "Well?"

"I took the train to Waxwood," Vivian said. "That's why I haven't been home for two days."

"I gathered that."

"I went to see Bertha."

"That old woman had no right to give you these letters, no right!" Larissa snarled.

"She didn't." Vivian's hands dug into her knees. "Evan's niece did."

"That Evan again," her mother grumbled.

"That Evan was Grandmother's lover." Vivian gazed at the narrowed face.

"You needn't put it so boldly, Vivian."

"Grandmother never loved Grandfather." She studied her mother. "You knew that, didn't you?"

"You believe what she says in the letters," her mother remarked. "But young ladies are apt to exaggerate, especially when it comes to love."

Vivian glared at her. "You think this is all quite amusing, don't you?"

"I'm not laughing, am I?" Larissa asked.

Vivian stared at the dark curtain. "She didn't love Grandfather, yet she married him and came back to San Francisco."

"Your grandmother was a sensible woman," her mother said. "Much too sensible to throw her life away on such a man as this Evan."

Vivian pushed the letters at her. "Have you forgotten what you've read already? It was Evan who withdrew the proposal."

"He must have had some scruples, then." Her mother sank down under the blanket.

"She needn't have married Grandfather," Vivian insisted. "Yet she did. How do you explain that?"

Larissa was silent for such a long time, Vivian thought she had no intention of answering. Then, as if shaken out of a memory, she said, "Your grandmother made mistakes, just as most women do when they're young and innocent."

"I don't think she was so innocent," Vivian said. "She may have been when she came to Waxwood, but not when she left."

"I refuse to entertain such a repulsive idea," Larissa growled. "She was my mother and your grandmother, after all." The last had a ring of desperation.

Vivian stared down at the pages on the bed. "What mistakes did she make?"

"I would think the letters make it rather obvious."

"That's precisely the point, Mother." Vivian placed her hands on the letters. "They make nothing obvious."

"Mistakes any young woman can make," said Larissa, "when she is given too much freedom."

Vivian eyed her. "Is that why you keep such a tight rein on mine?"

"That is why I hold you to such high standards," her mother corrected. Genuine hurt bled through the haughtiness. "You can behave in a foolhardy way sometimes, Vivian. I only want to protect you."

"Perhaps if I had something to love like Grandmother loved her art, I would be less foolhardy." Vivian looked toward the window. "I know very well you consider any serious attachment to a useful occupation for a lady more than just a mistake."

"It wasn't her attachment, it was what she did about it."

"You mean living in Brandywine?" Vivian asked.

"I mean involving herself with a fiend," her mother said. "Your grandmother, God rest her soul, was foolish in her youth. Thank goodness there were those who tried to keep her from it."

Vivian stared at her. "What do you mean?"

"Your great-grandfather was uneasy about her." Larissa folded her arms. "She says as much in the letters, doesn't she?"

"That was Grandfather's explanation," Vivian stiffened. "He has a fine way of making concern feel like an obligation."

"He was not obliged to come after her," Larissa pointed out. "He wouldn't have if he could have trusted his replacement."

"What replacement?"

"Evan, of course." Her mother sounded almost smug. "Flesa was such a close knit place. Everyone knew what had become of everyone else."

"What are you trying to say?"

"He knew Evan was living near Waxwood in that sinful colony."

"It was not sinful!"

"He went to see him."

Vivian's hands grew cold.

"He asked him to look after your grandmother." Larissa played with the lace edge of the blanket.

"Why would he ask a man he never liked to do that?"

"He thought he could trust him."

"What a devil Grandfather was!"

Larissa glared at her. "He was trying to protect her from herself. She was young and innocent and alone, and anything can happen to a lady under those circumstances. And he was glad to do it." There was a glint in her eye.

"What do you mean?"

"Your grandfather gave him money." Larissa sat back.

Vivian remembered the house with its compact lightness and its shutters and the roof Verina had been so proud of. "He built a house for his sister and niece."

"How touching." Larissa's tone was caustic.

"If Grandfather trusted him, why did he come to Waxwood himself?"

"Obviously, he didn't know he couldn't trust him until it was too late."

"Too late?"

Her mother sniffed. "You read the letters. This Evan took advantage of your grandmother's innocence."

"He fell in love with her," Vivian insisted.

Larissa looked away, but her voice was steady. "Your grandfather came just in time to save her."

"Save her?" Vivian laughed. "She was hardly a damsel in distress!"

"She was in distress," her mother asserted. "Evan took liberties with her and then dropped her as if she were a hot coal!"

"She wrote her mother that she was devastated," Vivian reminded her. "Not that she needed rescue."

"You've read so many French novels, you're beginning to sound like one," Larissa snapped.

"I've never read a French novel in my life," Vivian snapped back.

Her mother was quiet for a moment. "Your grandmother was about to become a social pariah. I should think that would require quite a savior."

"He saved her from being snubbed by the blue bloods?" Vivian asked warily.

"It was more than that, much more." Larissa preoccupied

herself with straightening the lace border of the blanket. "Your grandmother had her reputation to think of."

"Don't you think marriage is a rather extreme solution for off-hand gossip about a young lady who takes a year to herself in the country?" Vivian asked.

"I told you, it was much more than that."

Vivian stared at the wool blanket, her eyes blurry. "You mean — she didn't have a choice."

Her grandmother's words came back to her: *I must marry, I must marry somebody!*

Her mother's composed countenance tightened into a sculpture of lines, and her entire figure recoiled with disgust.

"I know what it means when a woman says she *must* marry," Vivian murmured.

Larissa's eyes remained on her a long time. "I never wanted you to know."

"Why?" Vivian asked. "Because the martyr in pink pearls was on her way to becoming a fallen woman?"

"Vivian!"

"She was not pure or artless. She was not the angel in the house." Her entire body shook with emotion. "She was a woman just like the rest of us."

"Yes. She was a foolish young woman who made one foolish mistake and almost made another," her mother said.

Vivian hesitated, then reached out her hand. "You won't go back now, will you, Mother? You'll tell me everything."

Larissa murmured. "Lot's wife looked back and turned into a pillar of salt, didn't she?" She looked at Vivian as if she were a ghost.

"You won't turn into salt," her daughter promised.

This seemed to compose Larissa, though her voice still wavered. "She knew by the end of June."

"It was why she was ill that summer," Vivian said.

"She went to see some woman doctor," said Larissa. "Even proper young ladies knew about such things back then."

Vivian looked down at the shiny folds in the blanket.

"Now perhaps you understand better," her mother said, pressing Vivian's hand, "why your grandfather did what he had to do."

Tears crept into Vivian's eyes. "What happened to the child?"

"She lost it, thank God."

"Thank God!" Vivian leapt up. "How can you be so cruel?"

"I'm cruel?" Her mother glared at her. "That foul, lecherous beast was the cruel one."

Vivian sank back on the bed, putting her head down. "Poor Grandmother."

"Your grandmother made quite good use of her opportunity," Larissa said in a tight voice. "She was the belle of San Francisco society in the sixties."

"And what else?" Vivian eyed her. She could not help feel her mother was holding something back.

"There is nothing else," Larissa insisted.

"Who told you all this? Grandmother?"

Larissa put the embroidery on the nightstand. "You ought to go to bed now, dear. We have a long day ahead of us tomorrow."

Vivian's nerves were coming apart. She watched her mother turn down the gas lamp on the bedside table and pulled the blanket to her chin as if she were a child afraid of the bogeyman.

"Grandfather told you, didn't he?" Vivian felt ill.

"I really am tired, dear."

"He told you about the love affair. He told you about the baby." She grabbed the blanket, flinging it to the floor.

"Vivian!"

"Did he make himself out to be the hero?" Her voice was shaking. "'There was a rascal after your mother, Risa, but the moment I showed her some regard, she folded like a paper doll.'"

"He said nothing of the kind!"

"'I saved her reputation, Risa, saved her from that oh so terrible man.'"

"Your grandfather did what he had to do."

Vivian held the bedpost, the room spinning around her. "You don't mean he had to marry Grandmother, do you? You mean something else."

Her mother did not answer.

"He gave him money," Vivian murmured. "Money to put Ebba in a decent place."

"Really, Vivian, it's time to go to bed," Larissa said in a stern voice.

Vivian studied her. "Did you know Evan's sister Ebba went mad shortly after Grandmother left?"

Her mother said, "I did not. But Father said she was unbalanced."

"She was in Glockpool Sanitarium," Vivian continued. "Verina says it's like a luxurious resort."

"What concern is that to us?"

"They had no money," she said. "They lived humbly at the colony. But suddenly they have money for an expensive sanitarium. Now why do you suppose that is?"

Larissa looked at her steadily. "You're playing games with me, Vivian."

The spider-like gaze made Vivian shiver. "I imagine Grandfather knows. Perhaps I ought to ask him."

Her mother said in a steely voice, "You won't ask him anything."

Vivian thought of the quivering old man whose eyes were so dazed and his outbursts filled with unrecognizable references. She knew her mother was right.

"How Grandfather must have painted a pretty picture when he told you," Vivian snarled. "The damsel in distress saved by the noble knight."

"That's not fair, Vivian. Your grandfather was always generous to her."

Vivian's throat grated. "Grandfather always loved a conquest story. Especially when he could make it his own."

"Your grandfather loved your grandmother very much. He's always loved her."

"He told you that too, I suppose?"

Her mother shuddered. "I never needed to ask."

"Perhaps you didn't. But I will." Vivian rose, ready to charge out.

Her mother grabbed her arm. "Your grandfather is in mourning, just like the rest of us. I will not have you disturbing him with your wild accusations. This is the limit, Vivian."

"I'm not a child, Mother."

"Then stop behaving like one!" Larissa finally broke, tears rising in her eyes.

"Perhaps Verina was right." She wavered. "I ought not to go chasing specters."

Her mother shuddered. "I don't know why you insist on this morbid idea."

"Morbid but true," Vivian said. "Phantoms and apparitions are all we've ever had of the Alderdices, Mother. They're all we'll ever leave our children and our grandchildren unless we face them and let them go."

Her mother fell back against the bed, her eyes wide and her breath short. She retrieved the blanket and arranged it on the bed. At that moment, Larissa looked like a child frightened by the monster in the closet, waiting for her father to come home and chase it away.

CHAPTER 36

*V*ivian stumbled into the hall. The ceiling pressed against her head and the ground looked as if it had no end at all. She suddenly heard sobs coming from her mother's room. They were not the uncontrollable sobs of grief but of exhaustion. She understood why. She forced Larissa to face a web of lies. There was nothing left for her but a vale of tears.

Vivian considered going back to comfort her. But she could not endure her mother's vulnerability just then.

She descended slowly down the stairs, her mind whirling. Basset had lit the hall lamp, and its wavering light threw a figure of a woman with long hair and a loose nightgown against the opposite wall. The features were hidden at first, but as Vivian's eyes adjusted, the chin appeared sharper, the eyelashes pointed, and the shoulders square. It looked like her grandmother. In her final months, Grandmother had drifted in the night calling out to imaginary servants. Grandfather had been afraid she would fall down the stairs, so he insisted she be moved to the first floor. It was there she had died.

Vivian felt for the letters in the pocket of her wrapper. Halfway down the hall, she found the room. Nothing had been altered since her grandmother died. The nightgown Grandmother had worn, a lovely chestnut silk with lace at the collar, lay over a chair as if she had just placed it there. The pillows were arranged so the first one leaning to the side just as her grandmother had liked it.

She closed her eyes to steady herself. The woman in the parlor portrait came to her mind, but the woman's features were now pointed as in the shadow she had just seen. There was a glint in the eyes too. She was seeing the specter of Penelope Alderdice, née Carlyle, the woman who had held liberty in her hands like a fragile bird but lost it in a betrayal that left her little choice but to crawl back into her cage, the sapphire necklace clasped tightly to her throat.

In her life now, she stood where her grandmother had the day she had arrived in Waxwood in 1852. She had been born to a legacy of entrapment. Could she escape it as Grandmother never had?

She opened her eyes. The letters were still scattered on the floor. She gathered them together and left the room. She climbed the stairs to the fourth floor, which contained only two rooms — a locked room, for which the key was lost, and the playroom.

The latter looked just as she and Jake had left it when they had played as children. She turned on the gaslight, and the yellow glare illuminated the small cupboard where the glass circus still stood, ready for its audience of delighted children. She felt for the panel at the bottom and pressed it back.

A large leather book lay in the secret place. Jake had found it and they had spent hours glancing through the old postcards and photographs from fifty years ago where the poses looked like corpses. They had made up stories about the torn ribbons, fragments of poems, tickets and programs someone had placed there. They named it the Alderdice Family Dream Book.

It was there she must bury the specter. She placed the letters in the book and secured the panel.

. . .

~~~~~

Author's Note
Welcome to the Waxwood Series!

THE BOOK you've just read went through some major transformations in terms of its genre. Simply put, "genre" refers to the type of story the book tells. For example, a cozy mystery tells a whodunit story (most of the time) solved by an amateur sleuth. A romance tells the story of boy meets girl (or girl meets girl or boy meets boy, depending on what story you're telling) that usually ends happily.

THIS BOOK IS a tale of historical fiction (meaning the story is set in an era in the past) — that goes without saying. But when I first published this book back in 2019 to launch the Waxwood Series, I labeled it as a family saga. At the time, I saw the series as a story of the decline of a Nob Hill family (the Alderdices) as the world around them changed.

BUT I HAVE since come to see that this series is really more about the coming-of-age of the main character (Vivian) as she maneuvers through the last decade of the 19th century. Like many young adults (and Vivian is eighteen here), she's trying to figure out the world around her and where she fits in (not an easy task when your world is being hurled into a whole new century). She's also trying to find her own identity when her family and the society she lives in imposes expectations on her about who she will be. Sounds like all of us in once we finished high school trying to figure out what we should do now, right?

.　.　.

I COME from the Middle East where young adults finish high school and immediately go into the army (even the women). After they finish the army, the next step is college, right? Not for many of these young people. It's almost a rite of passage for them to pack a bag and head for Southeast Asia or South America or some parts unknown to them and travel for a few months, living in youth hostiles and experiencing other cultures before they come home and settle down to finding a job or going to college. It's a way to give them the space and time they need to figure out where they stand in relationship to the world and what their future holds.

WHAT'S NEXT? Book 2 of this series is about Vivian's brother Jake and his own journey to self-discovery. Jake is only fifteen here, but in Book 2, he's already a young man and left with burdens on his shoulders. Turn the page to read an excerpt from the book!

HAPPY READING!
　　Tam

BOOK 2 INFORMATION

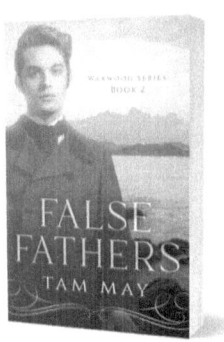

Waxwood, 1898: At nineteen, Jake Alderdice loses his grandfather, the only paternal figure he ever knew. His mother expects him to take his place as the new head of the family but Jake hardly has the qualities expected of a Gilded Age patriarch. He is contemplative rather than aggressive, hesitant instead of ambitious, and artistic rather than materialistic. And now, he has no one to guide him.

When the family fulfills Malcolm Alderdice's last request — to visit Waxwood, the coastal town where he wooed and won Penelope Alderdice — Jake befriends an older but illusive man prepared to teach him all he needs to know about Gilded Age manhood.

But is his new mentor all he claims to be? Or is he a wolf in sheep's clothing bent on leading Jake into a diabolical version of the Gilded Age man?

Will Jake discover the true meaning of Gilded Age masculinity or redefine it?

Read Book 2 of the series the Whispering Stories Book Blog called "historical fiction at its best!"

Read on for an excerpt from this book!

BOOK 2 EXCERPT

The day after the mourning ended, the curtains were drawn around the house. Alderdice Hall appeared luminous and airy again, the sun throwing patches of warmth onto the hardwood floors. As he dressed, his feeling of freedom turned into apprehension. He heard Vivian's words: *You must tell Mother.* He had turned twenty-one a few months before. Today was the beginning.

When he entered the dining room for breakfast, he found Larissa and his sister at their usual places, as if the two years in black had never been. His mother looked composed and detached in navy blue suit.

"Mother, you ought to wear cornflower blue." He greeted her with an airy peck above her cheek. "It's all right now, you know." He took his place beside his sister.

"That is no longer your place, Jacob," Larissa said. "You sit at the head of the table now."

He shrank back, staring at the chair elevated with cushions that had been his grandfather's.

"You're going to force him to sit in a dead man's place?" His sister stared.

"I don't intend to force him to do anything. I merely expect him to do his duty."

He removed the cushions and sat down. "Haven't I always done my duty?"

"I have no complaints against you on that score," she agreed.

"The implication being you have complaints against me," Vivian said with a wry smile. "Obedience was never my strong point, was it, Mother?"

Larissa gazed shrewdly at his sister. "Only recently, dear." Vivian looked away. His mother continued as he unfolded his napkin. "There are certain things we must discuss."

"Now that it's all over?" He licked his lips.

"All over with?" Larissa took up a cream-colored envelope that had come with the morning mail.

"Now that we can get on with our lives," Vivian said.

Larissa glared at her. "That's hardly respectful, Vivian."

"I'm only trying to be honest," she said. "Just like Grandmother was."

"There is such a thing as brutal honesty, Viv," Jake pointed out. "It's not very appropriate under the circumstances."

"Very true, Jacob." His mother gave him a satisfied look.

"But he's dead," Vivian said. "Surely, we're permitted to say the word now, just as we're permitted to wear bright colors and greet the sun."

Larissa's knife came crashing down on the floor. Basset, their butler retrieved it and returned to his place against the wall as discreet as ever.

"I'm sorry, Mother." Vivian paled. "I don't wish to upset you this morning."

"Vivian is only concerned for me, Mother," he said. "We never really discussed what would happen when I turned twenty-one."

"I suppose your grandfather didn't think—" His mother took a deep breath before continuing, "He told me several times how happy it would make him if you were to take your place in the business when you came of age."

"Don't you think it's a rather heavy burden to put an entire empire on a nineteen year old's shoulders?" Vivian asked.

"Your brother realizes he has a responsibility to the family."

Jake placed scrambled egg on his plate, but he had lost his appetite. "I wasn't intending to flounder about, Mother."

"I didn't think you were," she said. "And I didn't intend to put the entire empire on your shoulders, as your sister so picturesquely puts it." She gave his sister a shrewd look. "You shall begin at the beginning, just as your grandfather did."

"I respect Grandfather's wishes," said Jake. "But I don't think I would be good at business."

"Well, then?" She looked at him.

"I want to paint."

"Paint!"

"I mean I want to be an artist," he corrected. "A professional, successful, and *respected* artist."

He expected his mother to reject the idea, but she looked interested. "How do you expect to go about it?"

Her seriousness filled him with hope. "I'm not sure yet."

"Jake hasn't exactly had the chance to consider it," Vivian snapped. "We've all been locked up in this house, or have you forgotten, Mother?"

"I intend to devote this summer to finding out," he promised.

Larissa threaded her hands together. "I'm not entirely opposed to the idea, as long as you are respectable."

"I don't plan on disgracing the family," Jake mumbled.

"I just want to make sure you know what's expected of you, Jacob."

His sister let out a sour laugh. "Good Lord, you've been doing nothing but laying down expectations since we were born!"

"Those were the expectations of children," said Larissa. "Neither of you are children anymore."

Will Jake disgrace the Alderdice family? Or will he live up to his mother's expectations? You can find out by purchasing a copy of *False Fathers* at your favorite online bookstore at this link: https://tammayauthor.com/books-2/waxwood-series/false-fathers-waxwood-series-book-2.

How about that cool freebie I promised you? If you're into historical cozy mysteries featuring strong women who don't let society's rules about female behavior stop them from doing what they want, I urge you to check out the Adele Gossling Mysteries! Read on for how to get hold of the series' free novella, *The Missing Ruby Necklace*.

FREE NOVELLA

When a jewel and a girl go missing on New Year's Eve...

Eleanor McCarthy, a lovely though somewhat flighty debutante, has graced the tiny town of Arrojo, California, with her presence. One of Arrojo's prominent ladies throws a New Year's Eve shindig to introduce her to Arrojo's high society — whatever little of it there is. Naturally, the daughter and son of one of San

Francisco's influential lawyers, Adele and Jackson Gossling, are invited.

But screams replace popping champagne corks when Eleanor's priceless ruby necklace is discovered missing. And soon, so is Eleanor!

In this historical cozy mystery set in the early 20th century, follow Adele Gossling, stationary store owner and amateur sleuth, and her clairvoyant sidekick Nin Branch as they search for a ruby necklace that may or may not have been stolen and a young woman who may or may not have run away.

Want to read an excerpt from this book? I got you covered! Turn the page.

"Coffee!" Miss McCarthy laughed. "Heavens, no! I haven't had my first taste of champagne yet." She flung her hand out to her brother. "Bring me a bottle of champagne, my good man."

"I don't mind," he said.

Before he could saunter out the door, Mrs. Abberton jumped up. "I'll get it."

"I really think we ought to get coffee," Mr. Abberton mumbled.

"She wants champagne," Mrs. Abberton was almost stern. "It's a celebration, after all!" She practically fled from the room.

Adele followed her and caught her arm. She spoke in a soft tone. "Mrs. Abberton, why did Miss McCarthy faint?"

"She just told you, didn't she?" The woman gave a shrill laugh. "Albert said we ought to open some windows, but it was such a windy night, I —"

"It wasn't the windows," said Adele. "Or the corset."

"Of course it was!" The woman examined some bottles on the floor. "I never could read these labels."

"You were staring at Miss McCarthy as if something that wasn't there."

"What an imagination you have, dear." The woman said.

"Miss McCarthy had her hands on her throat when she fell," Adele continued. "You kept looking at her throat."

"Nonsense," the woman hissed.

"Miss McCarthy wasn't wearing her ruby necklace," Adele declared.

Mrs. Abberton tore through a row of bottles lying on a table. One rolled onto the floor with a crack and the bubbly drink spilled across the marble. She sunk into one of the chairs. "You're too observant, Miss Gossling."

"You saw it too."

"Just before the lights went out," she said. "But Eleanor is one of those girls who gets easily flustered with her jewelry. She says it weighs her down."

"If that's true, why were you so alarmed just now?" Adele said.

"I wasn't," the woman insisted. "She locks that necklace in a box. Albert tried to persuade her to put it in our safe at the finance company, but she refused."

"That's rather unusual," Adele said.

"Eleanor's a lovely girl, but rather flighty," The woman said in a harsh tone. "I expect Celestine spoils her."

"If the necklace is missing, there might be a theft involved," Adele suggested.

Jewelry goes missing all the time. But does that mean theft? And why is Mrs. Abberton so nervous?

How can you get your hands on a copy of *The Missing Ruby Necklace*, not available in any bookstore? Simple. Go to this link: https://landing.mailerlite.com/webforms/landing/l2u0c3. What else will you get when you get this novella? How about fun facts about women in history and true crime classic mysteries, which are just as fascinating, if not more so, as contemporary true crimes?

ABOUT THE AUTHOR

Writing has been Tam May's voice since the age of fourteen. She writes stories about powerful women set in the past. Her fiction gives readers a sense of justice for women, both the living and the dead. Tam's stories are set mostly around the Bay Area because she adores sourdough bread, Ghirardelli chocolate, and San Francisco history.

Tam is the author of the Adele Gossling Mysteries which take place in the early 20th century and features sassy suffragist and epistolary expert Adele Gossling whose talent for solving crimes doesn't sit well with the ideas of some people around her about women's place. Tam has also written historical fiction about women breaking loose from the confinements of their era.

Although Tam left her heart in San Francisco, she lives in the Midwest because it's cheaper. When she's not writing, she's devouring everything classic (books, films, art, music) and concocting yummy vegan dishes.

Tam May can be reached at:
WEBSITE: http://tammayauthor.com/
EMAIL: tammay70@tammayauthor.com
FACEBOOK: https://www.facebook.com/tammayauthor
INSTAGRAM: https://www.instagram.com/tammayauthor/
PINTEREST: https://www.pinterest.com/tammayauthor/